The Cowboy Sheriff

TRISH MILBURN

D0180603

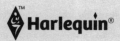

TORONTO NEW YORK LONDON
AMSTERDAM PARIS SYDNEY HAMBURG
STOCKHOLM ATHENS TOKYO MILAN MADRID
PRAGUE WARSAW BUDAPEST AUCKLAND

Recycling programs
for this product may
not exist in your area.

ISBN-13: 978-0-373-75407-6

THE COWBOY SHERIFF

Copyright © 2012 by Trish Milburn

"You want to be a cowgirl?

"If so, you're going to have to learn how to ride a horse." Simon began bouncing his leg as he held the baby firmly. Hannah laughed.

After a couple of minutes, he noticed Keri standing in the doorway.

"Look, Hannah, it's your aunt Keri."

A hint of a smile tugged at the edges of Keri's mouth. Then, as if she realized what she'd done, her lips formed a humorless line.

"Why are you doing this?" she asked.

"Because once upon a time we were friends, and I'd like to be again."

He braced himself for a hot and sharp response, but it didn't come. Keri simply stood in the doorway for a few seconds then turned to head back to work.

He wasn't about to examine why, but her response made him smile. Sure, they'd been friends before and the whole deal with her brother was long past due for resolution. But those weren't the only reasons he was determined to place himself back in Keri Mehler's life.

He was attracted to her, and no one was more surprised than him.

"So, what do you think, Hannah? Think I have a shot?"

Dear Reader,

I hope you've been enjoying The Teagues of Texas trilogy and falling in love with those handsome cowboy brothers. In *The Cowboy Sheriff*, oldest brother, Simon, finally finds the woman who will put his serial dating ways to rest forever—and she's been under his nose the entire time.

I'm a big fan of stories where friends fall in love, and this one has a twist. Friends become enemies become lovers. Simon and Keri have a winding road to their happily-ever-after, but I think that makes it all that much sweeter.

I'd love to hear what you think of the Teague brothers and their stories. You can find me on Facebook, Twitter and my website at www.trishmilburn.com. Hope to hear from you soon.

Trish

ABOUT THE AUTHOR

Trish Milburn wrote her first book in the fifth grade and has the cardboard-and-fabric-bound, handwritten and colored-pencil-illustrated copy to prove it. That "book" was called *Land of the Misty Gems,* and not surprisingly it was a romance. She's always loved stories with happy endings, whether those stories come in the form of books, movies, TV programs or marriage to her own hero.

A print journalist by trade, she still does contract and free-lance work in that field, balancing those duties with her dream-come-true career as a novelist. Before she published her first book, she was a finalist eight times in the prestigious Golden Heart contest sponsored by Romance Writers of America, winning twice. Other than reading, Trish enjoys traveling (by car or train—she's a terra firma girl!), watching TV and movies, hiking, nature photography and visiting national parks.

You can visit Trish online at www.trishmilburn.com. Readers also can write to her at P.O. Box 140875, Nashville, TN 37214-0875.

Books by Trish Milburn
HARLEQUIN AMERICAN ROMANCE
1228—A FIREFIGHTER IN THE FAMILY
1260—HER VERY OWN FAMILY
1300—THE FAMILY MAN
1326—ELLY: COWGIRL BRIDE
1386—THE COWBOY'S SECRET SON*
1396—COWBOY TO THE RESCUE*

*The Teagues of Texas

To Kim Law, Lara Hansen and Gretchen Stull—
my awesome brainstorming buddies.
Thanks for the titles.

Chapter One

Simon Teague eyed the radar image on his computer and groaned.

"Colorful," said Deputy Pete Kayne as he walked behind Simon with a fresh cup of coffee.

"Little too colorful." The image showed too much blue and pink for his taste. If the snow and, worse, ice dipped down much farther, they were going to have a devil of a night.

"I heard on the way in that they think at least the ice will stay north."

Simon grunted. It was bad enough when Dallas and Fort Worth got socked with winter weather. On the rare occasion that it ventured as far south as Austin, San Antonio and the Hill Country where they now sat, people tended to freak out as if the apocalypse had arrived. That led to wrecks, which led to his deputies and him spending miserable hours out in the cold.

He'd just clicked on the hourly forecast when the phone rang. He reached for the receiver as he scrolled through temperatures that should never cross the Red River into Texas.

"Sheriff's Department."

"May I speak to Sheriff Teague?"

"Speaking." Simon minimized the computer screen and shifted his focus fully to the phone call.

"This is James Dial with the Dallas P.D."

"Just saw you all are getting slammed up there."

"Yeah, that's why I'm calling," Dial said, sounding serious.

A chill went down Simon's back. This wasn't going to be good.

Dial took a deep breath before continuing. "I just got back from a crash scene, two deaths. Next of kin for one of the deceased is listed as living in Blue Falls, but I've been unable to make contact. Probably better coming from someone local, anyway, though it's going to be awful either way."

Damn, of everything his job entailed, telling relatives someone they loved had died was the absolute worst. He'd rather break up a thousand bar fights, even take a few punches himself, than have to make one next-of-kin call.

"Who are you trying to contact?"

"Keri Mehler."

A rush of cold washed through Simon. His first thought was of Carter, Keri's brother and his once-upon-a-time best friend. But then the fact that Dial was calling from Dallas registered. Keri's older sister and her family lived in Dallas.

"Sammi?"

"Samantha and Benjamin Spencer died at the scene when their SUV flipped and rolled several times."

Simon gripped the phone harder. "The baby?" He'd last seen the little girl at the Fourth of July celebration as she crawled around on a blanket next to the lake while her parents, Keri and the rest of Blue Falls had waited for the fireworks to start. He swallowed hard at the idea that she'd been killed, too, before reaching her first birthday.

"Scared, but not a scratch on her," Dial said. "It's a miracle considering how bad that vehicle looked."

Simon ran his fingers through his hair. How was he going to tell Keri, after everything she'd been through?

"I take it you know Ms. Mehler?"

"Yeah." Had known her nearly all his life, had once been her friend. Had spent nearly as much time at her house when he was growing up as he had his own.

"Then you can make contact?"

Simon made an affirmative sound, then cleared his throat. "I'll head over there now."

"Until Ms. Mehler can come to pick her up, Hannah Spencer is being held in state care."

Poor little girl. The image of her crying for her mother, a mother who'd never be able to hold her again, twisted Simon's gut.

After he wrote down all the particulars, Simon hung up and ran his hand over his face. When he looked up, Pete and Anne Marie Wallace, the 9-1-1 dispatcher, were staring at him, both with tight, pinched looks of concern on their faces.

"Keri Mehler's sister and brother-in-law died in a car accident tonight."

Anne Marie gasped and lifted her hand to her mouth.

"Keri's niece?" Pete asked.

"She's fine." Simon shook his head slowly. "God, I hate doing this." He stood and walked toward the coatrack by the door.

"Want me to go with you?" Pete asked, not sounding particularly anxious but willing to help out nonetheless.

"No, you stay here in case the weather gets worse and the crap hits the fan. Don't know how long I'll be gone. Call in Jack or Connor if you need to."

After slipping on his heavy ranch coat and tan Stetson, Simon stepped out into the cold night to deliver even colder news.

WAS THAT A SNOWFLAKE? Keri moved toward the bakery's front window and pressed her face close to it. Sure enough, a few snowflakes drifted through the crisp night air. A girlish thrill zipped through her. She hadn't seen snow in Blue Falls in more than a decade and only twice in her lifetime. Both times didn't amount to much but still enough to scrape together the world's smallest snowmen. When she'd been twelve, she'd managed to gather enough snow to make a little snow family—Mom, Dad, two kids and even a snow dog. Of course, they'd all been about the height of a saltshaker and had lasted less than a day, but they'd been fun nonetheless.

She shifted her gaze across the street. Most of Main Street was already closed up for the evening, with the exception of the Frothy Stein. It'd take more than a swipe from Old Man Winter to part the regulars from their whiskey and Shiner Bock.

She'd been imagining curling up in front of her fireplace with a big mug of hot chocolate and a book from her teetering to-be-read pile for the past hour. But first, she had to finish cleaning the bakery. At least Sunshine Monroe, her second in command, had finished the prep for the next morning's baking before she'd had to leave to pick up her son from basketball practice.

Keri hummed along with the tune by Lady Antebellum as she returned to the mop and bucket of soapy water. After she made a couple of swipes, she was startled by knocking on the front door.

She froze when she saw Simon Teague standing on the other side of the glass. What the devil could he want? She pointed at the obvious sign hanging on the door. "We're closed."

He didn't go away. And something about the solemn look on his face caused her heart to skip a beat. What kind of trouble had Carter gotten into this time? And why the hell did Simon feel he had to be the one to tell her? It still irked her every time she saw him in uniform. Sure, everyone else in town seemed to love him to pieces, but she couldn't see past what he'd allowed to happen to her brother, his supposed best friend. Even Carter had told her to let it go, but she'd never been the kind to forgive and forget. Not wanting to be angry every time she saw him, she'd settled into a sort of detachment as if she barely knew him.

She propped the mop against the edge of the front counter and strode toward the door. Why had she fantasized about a cozy night at home? That was like screaming at Murphy and his damn law to come screw stuff up.

When she unlocked the door and opened it a fraction, the blast of cold air smacked her in the face.

"Little late for a doughnut, isn't it?" she asked, not relinquishing her hold on the edge of the door.

He didn't toss a snappy comeback her way or offer up one of the smiles that he had to know annoyed her. The fact he wasn't acting normal worried her more than his unexpected appearance outside the bakery.

"Can I come in?"

She wanted to say "no" and ignore the very bad feeling pooling in her middle. Instead, she took a step back and opened the door wide enough for him to fit through. Once he was inside, she shut the door on the unholy cold and crossed her arms across her chest.

"Is it Carter?"

Simon had removed his hat and picked at the edge of

the brim without looking. He shifted from one leg to the other then nodded at the tables to his right. "Let's sit."

"No, thanks. Just come on out with whatever it is you think my brother has done this time."

Simon winced. If she hadn't been watching him closely, she wouldn't have noticed.

"It's not Carter."

"Then what?" She paused and reminded herself to not get so irritated. "I've still got work to do before I can go home. And I'd like to head out soon since it's snowing."

The discomfort tugging at the lines of his face sent another surge of worry through her, making her wish she'd ignored his presence out on the sidewalk. Instinct told her she didn't want to hear whatever he'd come to tell her.

"A few minutes ago, I received a call from Dallas P.D. Sammi was in an accident."

She went still, not even sure her lungs were pumping air.

"Is she okay?" The words came out in a ragged whisper.

Simon stood silent for a moment too long, a moment in which she grasped the terrible truth of what he was going to say next. Her mind screamed at her to flee. If she didn't hear the words, they wouldn't be true.

"I'm so sorry Keri. She and Ben were both killed."

She stared at Simon without really seeing him. He was no more than a hulking blur in a world suddenly gone very dark. It took so much effort to form a single word.

"Both?"

Simon took a step forward, and his footfalls on the floor sounded so much louder than they actually were, like the booming of cannons instead of the normal tread of boots. Keri retreated away from his outstretched hand. She couldn't let him touch her. If he made contact, she'd know he was real, that what he'd said wasn't just part of a horrendous nightmare. She could convince herself that she was really already at home, curled up in that chair in front of the fire asleep.

From somewhere beyond the disbelief, she managed to find the breath to utter another word. "Hannah?" As soon as she asked, she hated herself. She didn't want to know, couldn't imagine going on in a world where that precious little girl had died before seeing her first Christmas.

"She's fine, no injuries."

She collapsed into a chair and latched onto that one glimmer of good news among an ocean of bad. "Where is she?"

"In state custody until you can arrive."

It took several seconds for the words to travel from her eardrum to the part of her brain that actually understood. Memories jerked her back more than a year, to when she and Sammi had sat on Keri's front porch enjoying the pleasant October air.

"I have a favor to ask you," Sammi had said as she ran a hand over her slight baby bump.

"Sure."

"Ben and I are drawing up legal documents, and we want to name you as the baby's guardian should anything happen to us."

"Nothing's going to happen to you. You're both healthy as a horse."

"You know things happen unexpectedly sometimes." Like their parents dying within a year of each other, both from cancer. "Ben's parents already love this child, but they can't take on raising a baby."

The Spencers were wonderful people, but they were already in their seventies. Ben was their only child, born after they'd given up on having children.

Oh, God, they'd just lost their only child. Something about the brutality of that pain hit Keri more than her own.

Simon bent down in front of her, but he didn't say something asinine like, "Are you okay?" She almost wished he would so she could get angry and scream at him. She wanted to kill the messenger, do something that would fill the growing emptiness, show some emotion before her mind shut down and forgot how.

He didn't touch her, but she got the impression he was there to catch her if she suddenly fell over. Normally, that would make her mad, Simon Teague thinking she needed saving. Really, anyone thinking she needed saving. But tonight wasn't normal, was it?

They sat in silence, the only sounds the drone of the heating unit running and the whistle of the wind around the edge of the building. After what seemed like hours, Simon was the one to speak first.

"It's too dangerous to drive up there tonight, but we can go in the morning."

His words made no sense. Go where? Why would he be going anywhere with her?

"Keri?" When his hand came to rest atop hers in her lap, she jerked as if he'd hit her with a branding iron.

Keri snatched her hand away and felt tears burn her eyes. Hot, searing tears that would surely make her go blind. "No, you're wrong. I don't believe it."

It was the way Simon sat without speaking, how his expression continued to convey sorrow that broke through her final denial. Her fight dissolved and her chin trembled, but she somehow held her tears back. If she fell apart, she'd never be able to find and reassemble all the pieces.

She pushed her chair back, away from him and the

truth written all over his face. When she stood, her legs shook so much she expected to fall into a heap on the floor. She walked over and grabbed the mop and bucket of dirty water. As she carried them to the utility room and set about dumping the water down the drain and rinsing the mop, she sensed Simon in the doorway. She ignored him as she finished her work then headed for her coat and purse.

She flicked off the lights to the kitchen and made for the front door. Simon caught her arm halfway there.

"Where are you going?"

"To Dallas."

"Not tonight."

"Yes, tonight. My niece needs me."

He increased the pressure on her arm enough to make her look up at him. "Yes, she does. But she needs you alive."

She wanted to ignore him, but a voice deep inside her acknowledged he was right. She couldn't be so reckless, not for her own sake but for Hannah's.

"Go home, Keri. Pull together whatever you need. I'll pick you up first thing in the morning."

"I can drive myself."

"Not in that little car of yours. The roads are really bad in Dallas."

She let her breath out in a long, shaky sigh. "I said I wouldn't go tonight."

"I heard you. Your car won't be any more capable tomorrow. And I don't want you behind the wheel that far, anyway."

Damn it, why couldn't he just leave? He'd done his duty. She glared at him, holding on to her frustration so she didn't have to think about the other emotions grasping at her like claws. Not seeing any other alternative, she said, "Fine," then headed toward the door.

She waited for him to step outside so she could lock up. Before she could flee to her little Honda, he stepped into her path.

"Promise me you won't go anywhere tonight."

"I'm just going home." She pushed past him so he couldn't see the tears building and threatening to spill down her cheeks.

When she sank into the driver's seat of her car, she had to bite her lip to keep it from trembling. She blinked hard to clear her eyes, swiping at an errant tear. She couldn't start crying or she might never stop.

She started the car and began the short drive to her house, the house she'd grown up in, where the three Mehler siblings had done homework and had parties and chased their shepherd mix, Trigger, trying to lasso him as if he was a wild horse.

"Oh, Sammi," she said, choking on the words.

A glance in her rearview mirror revealed that Simon was following her, making sure she didn't hightail it straight to Dallas. She gripped the steering wheel until her knuckles popped. Ironic that he was the one concerned about her lying.

She pulled into her driveway and walked inside without even looking in his direction. As soon as she closed the door and turned on the light, she heard him drive away.

And then all the memories filling the house rushed her. Their mom making strudel in the kitchen, their dad watching UT football games in the living room, Carter and Simon snickering about whatever boys snicker about, Sammi and her playing one on one in the driveway.

Sammi talking on the phone with friends.

Sammi getting ready for her prom date with Brad Fisher.

Sammi packing to leave for college.

Keri clamped a hand over her mouth to muffle a cry and slid down the door to the floor.

She had no idea how long she sat there, not crying but merely staring into space and trying to remember every moment of Sammi's life. How could she be gone? Keri held out hope that this was all just a dream, one that felt way too real.

At some point, she struggled to her feet and started roaming from one room to another, trailing her hand over family photos, an afghan made by her mother, the blue faux granite countertops Keri had installed the previous year. When she ended up at the room she'd shared with Sammi, she couldn't step inside. Since she now slept in the master bedroom, she didn't come in here often. Now she didn't know if she'd ever be able to enter the room again.

She closed the door on the past and went back downstairs to her own room. For a long time, she'd avoided moving into the master suite she'd always thought of as her parents' domain. Only after she'd totally redone the bedroom and adjoining bathroom and gotten different furniture had she been able to call it hers and not feel as though she was invading their space.

Tonight it offered no comfort as she strode in and sank onto the side of her bed. Though she was tired, she knew herself well enough to know she wasn't going to sleep a wink. If not for the crippling ice in Dallas, she'd be on the road. And to hell with Simon Teague's concerns.

She spent the hours of the night packing, calling Sunshine to make arrangements for the operation of the bakery while she was gone and drinking countless cups of coffee. She even tried to go to bed only to discover she'd been right in the first place. She couldn't sleep despite how her mind wanted to power down.

By the time dawn revealed the snow hadn't amounted to more than the equivalent of a heavy frost, she was sitting next to her bags in the living room. She heard Simon's department-issue SUV as soon as it turned onto her street. She had the front door locked and was down the steps before he pulled into her driveway.

He handed her a thermal mug of coffee, and she took it without a word. What was there to say? She could think of a dozen people with whom she'd rather be riding, but she didn't want to put anyone else in danger on slick roads. She desperately wished she didn't have to make the trip at all.

For a couple of hours, they made good time. But around Hico, they ran into the southern edge of the ice storm's path. Simon had to slow down more with each mile they traveled until it felt as if they were barely moving. At this pace, it was going to take forever to reach Dallas and Hannah.

Keri found herself leaning forward and gripping the edge of her seat. Layers of ice bent tree limbs and caused power lines to swoop. Smoke poured out of chimneys, and she wondered if that was because the electricity and thus the heat were out. She hoped wherever Hannah was, she was warm and safe.

"Hard to believe something so pretty can be so dangerous," Simon said.

They'd been quiet so long that the sound of his voice startled her. She couldn't decide if the strained silence or talking to him was worse.

"Yeah." That solitary word was all she could muster.

As the miles slowly ticked by, she glanced at Simon's

profile. He looked tense, and she wondered how much effort it was taking him to creep along at such an agonizing pace and to keep the SUV from sliding off into a ditch.

She bit her lip and stared out her side window, trying to bar the image of Ben and Sammi's vehicle spinning out of control. Why had they been out in the storm, anyway? A surge of anger made her want to pound her fists into something hard and immovable. Sammi was smart, so why had she made such a stupid move? Why had she gotten herself killed?

Keri realized she might never get the answers to those questions, and that left her feeling even more bereft.

Their progress was so slow that she'd swear she could swim through taffy faster. By the time they reached the outskirts of Dallas, she was a ball of knotted muscles and blistering fatigue. Once in the city, the streets got marginally better. The sun was out and actually melting a bit of the accumulated ice.

When Simon finally pulled into a parking lot outside of a Dallas P.D. precinct, she let some of her tense muscles relax. They'd made it. But then she wasn't sure if she had the strength to haul herself to her feet and inside.

"Keri?"

For some reason, the sound of Simon's deep voice surprised her again.

"What?"

He looked across the vehicle at her. "Have you been able to reach Carter?"

She gripped the door handle so hard she was in danger of ripping it off. "No." She refrained from reminding Simon that were it not for him, her brother might be with her now. She spurred her tired body into movement and got out of the SUV before Simon could ask any more questions she didn't want to answer.

She'd tried Carter the night before only to discover the last number she had for him no longer worked. He was out there somewhere unaware that his oldest sister had died.

And it was all Simon Teague's fault.

Chapter Two

Simon watched Keri as she and Ben's parents handled the heartbreaking details of being next of kin. Her actions and responses were mechanical, like an autopilot program without a shred of emotion. He'd known her nearly their entire lives and felt he'd never known her less.

Keri Mehler had always been one part girl, one part ball of fire. Didn't matter if she was making moves on the basketball court in high school, yanking her younger brother into line or telling Simon to take a soaring nose-dive off the nearest bridge, she always did everything full out. But now? Now the fire was nowhere to be found, replaced by a detachment as cold as the ice that coated the world outside.

Would he be any different if he ever lost Nathan or Ryan?

But Keri's new reality was even worse. She'd lost almost her entire family. All she had left was a brother who was God only knew where and a baby who'd lived a miracle and a tragedy in the same moment. A baby who would grow up looking to Keri to be her mother.

The door on the opposite side of the room opened and a woman who was probably with Child Protective Services walked in holding a sleeping Hannah. Keri stared without moving for so long that tension and awkwardness began to rob the room of air. The woman with Hannah in her arms shifted her gaze to him.

"She's been fed and changed," she said. "And we have some supplies for you—diapers, wipes, food. Car seat, too."

He nodded then glanced at Keri again. He didn't think he'd ever seen anything sadder, emptier. It was as though everything that made her who she was had simply disappeared as if it'd never existed.

Not wanting the woman or anyone with Dallas P.D. to think Keri wasn't fit to care for Hannah, he started toward the little girl. Keri moved in the same instant, crossing the room to take the only part of Sammi that remained. Though she ran her fingertips across Hannah's cheek, Keri's expression didn't change.

The other woman placed a hand on Keri's shoulder. "I'm very sorry for your loss."

"Thank you," Keri said, her voice as hollow as an empty bucket. She pulled Hannah closer and walked out of the room.

The lady from CPS gave Simon a worried look. "Is she going to be okay?"

He nodded. "Eventually. Just a shock."

"I can imagine. Does she have help?"

He hesitated a moment. "A brother, friends." Of course the brother was so off the radar that he didn't even know his oldest sister was dead yet. But Simon was banking on Keri snapping out of her dazed state and giving her niece all the love and care she could muster. She'd never do anything less. Sammi wouldn't have named Keri guardian if she hadn't believed her sister could handle the responsibility.

By the time he reached the corridor, Keri was already

at the door to the parking lot. He grabbed the car seat sitting on the floor and followed her.

Without speaking, they worked together to get first the car seat and then Hannah settled into the back of the Tahoe before she froze. As they snapped the seat belt into place, Hannah's eyes opened. She blinked her bright blue eyes a few times before letting out a wail that would wake the comatose.

Keri jerked back and stared at her niece. Simon was worried he'd been wrong about her being able to care for Hannah, but then something seemed to register in her mind. She dug in the diaper bag until she found a pacifier, a very girly pink one with a flower design on the end.

"Look what I found," she said to Hannah as she waved the pacifier in front of the little girl's grasping hands. She allowed Hannah to snatch the pacifier and shove it into her mouth.

Keri smoothed Hannah's wispy blond hair with a gentleness he didn't know she possessed. His breath caught midway through an exhalation. Why had that simple gesture moved something inside him, something way too darn close to his heart?

He shook his head and made his way to the driver's seat. "We better get to the hotel before the streets get slick again." No way was he driving on frozen roads with a baby in the car, one who'd already cheated death once.

They all were due some sleep. He'd slept like crap the night before, and he doubted that sorrow and anger had let Keri sleep, either.

And it was the God's honest truth that he needed to get away from her for a few minutes to let the wildly inappropriate and unexpected sliver of attraction he'd felt toward her fade away. To let his common sense make a reappearance and remind him that what he was feeling was no more than sorrow for her loss, for all her losses.

Even the one for which she still blamed him.

KERI WANTED TO RUN AWAY. Maybe if she moved fast enough, she could outrun the past. And if she headed in the right direction, maybe she could bring Sammi back. Her mom. Her dad. Life before Carter went down the wrong path.

Her jaw clenched at that thought, especially considering who was sitting next to her. She stared out the side window at the frozen landscape instead of at Simon Teague. If she looked at him now, it would only add to the pain ripping her to shreds inside. She felt like wailing but that would wake up Hannah, who'd fallen back to sleep as Simon eased the car along the dark and largely deserted streets. Ice hung heavy from trees and the edges of the buildings they passed, and she had no doubt that black ice lurked on the dark surfaces of the streets where what had melted during the day had refrozen.

People with any sense weren't out in these kinds of conditions. But then most people didn't have to pick up their orphaned niece and make arrangements for their sister's funeral.

She swallowed the jagged, lemon-size lump in her throat, pushed away the need to fall completely apart. She didn't have that luxury. Hannah needed her. Plus, Simon was the last person she wanted seeing her turn into a blubbering mess.

The only reason she was allowing him to chauffeur her around was the complete and utter lack of options. Though it had galled her to accept his help, she'd convinced herself he was just doing his job, ensuring the safety of the citizens of Blue Falls. And despite the haze of pain, she had enough sense to know she shouldn't be driving on icy roads in her current state.

The Spencers had offered to let her stay with them, probably more because they didn't want to be parted from Hannah than anything, but Keri couldn't face being trapped inside four walls with that kind of deep sorrow. She had enough of her own to carry without exposing herself to even more. She couldn't crack, and witnessing that kind of raw loss might just do the cracking.

Some people looked to fate as a shining beacon of hope. She knew better. Fate was a cruel, heartless bitch who did nothing but take.

Just as she was thinking fate was probably getting extra giggles out of the fact that Keri had been left with no one better than Simon Teague to turn to, he pulled into the parking lot for the hotel.

As he switched off the engine, she hopped out of the car, eager to have some space between them. She had Hannah unbuckled and the carrier removed from the car seat base by the time Simon reached the back of the SUV for their bags. She had to give him credit for one thing— he wasn't forcing her to talk. This streak of silence had to be some sort of record for him.

Normally, he'd talk to anyone about anything. Didn't matter if it was politics with the morning coffee crowd at the Primrose Café or feigning lovesickness amongst the members of the local Red Hat Society. She'd even seen him wink at Girl Scouts selling cookies, making them giggle and hide their faces in embarrassment. Though she doubted even he could find an opening for teasing or flirting in their current situation.

As she carefully placed her feet one in front of the other on the icy parking lot, Simon hurried up next to her.

"I can carry her."

"I'm okay." She shifted the carrier to her side and gripped the handle firmly.

Simon strode ahead then held the hotel's door open for her. She mumbled a thank-you without meeting his eyes, then stepped into the warmth of the lobby. She scanned the grouping of cushy chairs next to a faux fireplace and a rack full of tourist brochures as Simon headed for the registration desk.

Hannah woke and began to fuss. Did she know her mother was gone? Would her crying get worse the longer Sammi didn't make an appearance?

Keri shook her head. She couldn't think about that now, couldn't think about anything more than the next few minutes. By the time she dug Hannah's bottle out of the diaper bag, Simon had them all checked into the hotel.

He nodded to his right, then headed down the corridor. "I got you a room at the end of the hall with mine next door," he said.

What he didn't say made her pause for a moment. Was he positioning himself as a shield between a potentially cranky baby and the rest of the guests on the floor? That seemed even more likely when she realized that there wasn't a room across the hall from hers, just the doorway to the stairs leading to the upper floors.

Simon used one of the key cards to open her door and waited for her to enter the room before carrying in her bags. After he placed them in the corner, he turned toward her and extended the key.

"Would you like something to eat?" he asked.

"No. I'm not hungry." That wasn't exactly true. Her stomach had been grumbling like a bear for several hours, but she didn't think food and the spinning in her middle could coexist for long.

Keri took the key card to her room, but Simon made

no move to leave. When she looked up, she realized she hadn't been this close to him in years. They crossed paths, of course. Hard not to in a town the size of Blue Falls. But they weren't exactly dance partners at the music hall. She'd forgotten just how blue his eyes were, a striking blue-gray.

She swallowed against the memory from when they were fourteen and she'd finally acknowledged to herself that he was passably cute. Not that she'd ever in a million years admit that to anyone else, least of all Simon. She'd rather run through a cactus patch naked.

It'd been one of those sticky hot days. After a baseball game in which Simon and Carter's team had trounced a team from Fredericksburg, they'd had a party at her house. Pizza, sodas and cold slices of watermelon. And a surreptitious game of spin the bottle. She'd just taken her turn and landed on Simon when her mother had figured out what they were doing and put a stop to it. His lips remained a mystery.

At the time she'd been secretly disappointed, though she'd feigned relief. Two years later, she'd counted herself lucky.

And yet she couldn't deny his eyes were just as enticing now as they'd been across that empty bottle.

Simon broke eye contact first, snapping her back to the present. He shifted his gaze to where she'd placed Hannah and her carrier on the bed.

"If you need anything, just call or knock on my door," he said.

"We're fine." She tried to sound stronger than she felt, but she just ended up sounding like a wasp set on stinging. Still, she kept going. "You don't even have to stay. We'll ride back with Sunshine after..." She swallowed hard. "After the funeral." Keri strode toward the door and held it open for him. She had no room in her cluttered and bruised thoughts for memories of a stupid, juvenile crush. Had no idea why that particular memory had chosen this of all moments to float to the surface.

This time, Simon didn't hesitate. He walked out the door without another word. She closed her door before he could even slip the key into his. As if on cue, Hannah began to cry.

THREE HOURS LATER, SIMON returned to the hotel with two barbecue dinners. He heard Hannah's cries as soon as he turned into their corridor. Sounded like his plan of putting them at the end of the hallway wasn't going quite as planned.

He had to knock twice before Keri came to the door, a red-faced and teary Hannah propped on her hip. Keri looked as if she was at the end of her rope. Without even asking for an invitation, he edged his way into the room and closed the door behind him.

After setting the bag of food on the little round table, he held out his arms. "Let me have her."

"I've got her."

"Keri." He waited until she met his eyes, refusing to give in to her inherent stubbornness and determination to do everything on her own. "Let me give you a break."

She hesitated a moment before shifting Hannah toward him. Even after he had a firm hold on the child, she didn't let go.

"I won't drop her," he said gently. It felt odd to speak to her that way, so unlike their friendly teasing from years ago or the thinly veiled animosity of more recent years.

Finally, she let go and sank onto the edge of the bed.

"I can't get her to calm down. What if she never stops crying?"

"She will." Eventually, Hannah would get used to seeing Keri's face instead of her mother's. A profound sadness welled within him at the thought that someday, maybe not that far in the future, Hannah would forget her parents entirely.

He bounced Hannah softly in his arms as he watched Keri close her eyes and run her hands through her hair. The way the strands were sticking out, it wasn't the first time her hair had gotten that treatment tonight.

When Keri opened her eyes again, he nodded toward the bag on the table. "You need to eat."

"I just want to sleep. It feels like ages since I slept."

"Food first. You haven't eaten all day."

She gave him an odd look, as though she couldn't believe he'd noticed. That or she really hadn't realized she'd had nothing but a couple of bottles of water since before he'd arrived at the bakery with the horrible news about the accident. Whatever she was thinking, she heaved herself off the bed and over to the table. She sank into one of the chairs and opened the box.

He turned his attention to Hannah and bopped her nose gently with his index finger. "Now there, little missy. Let's see if we can figure out something to do besides crying." He carried her over to where he'd tossed a second bag into the chair opposite Keri and pulled out a stuffed bunny he'd found at the Walmart next to the barbecue place. "Look at what I found," he said in that goofy, higher pitched voice that adults seemed predisposed to use around babies. He wiggled it in front of Hannah, using one of its floppy ears to tickle her nose.

Hannah let out another cry, albeit a bit halfhearted, then a sniffle before it all was replaced with a smile as she grabbed the bunny.

"Where did that come from?" Keri asked before shoving a fry in her mouth.

"I'm guessing China." He consulted the tag on the rabbit's fuzzy behind. "Yep, China."

He glanced over at Keri and saw an all-too-familiar annoyance on her face. This time, he didn't mind it. Anything was better than the terrible blankness. They weren't friends anymore, but that didn't mean he wanted to see her that damaged.

"So, what shall we call this guy?" he asked Hannah as he placed her on the bed and he lay on his side next to her. Though her face was still flushed and tear-stained, she'd done a complete one-eighty. Now she giggled and flapped the bunny's ears up and down, making it look as if it was going to take off in flight.

Keri shoved her chair away from the table. "She needs to eat, too. I tried to feed her earlier, but she wouldn't stop crying long enough."

Simon put up a hand to stop her. "You keep eating. I'll feed her."

Keri gave him a raised eyebrow. "You know how to feed a baby?"

"Can't be that hard. Plus, I've got to get in some practice. Going to have a new niece of my own soon. And I plan to be her favorite uncle."

Keri snorted, and it sounded so much like the normal her that he felt some hope she would get through this. "If the kid's smart, she'll pick Ryan for that."

Simon shifted his attention to Hannah, who was now jabbering with her new best friend. "Can you believe that, Hannah? You'll vouch for me, won't you?"

Hannah gave him a wide grin that melted his heart. She really was a cute little thing. It broke his melted heart to think of all she'd lost without even knowing it.

He managed to keep Keri eating and Hannah from crying over the next few minutes as he fed the little girl. When Hannah had eaten the last of her green beans and applesauce, he noticed Keri was leaning on one of her hands with her eyes closed.

"You need to get some sleep."

She opened her eyes slowly as though it was difficult to force her eyelids into compliance. "I'll sleep when she does."

"I'll take care of her." She opened her mouth to protest further. "Listen. I know you don't like this, but for right now let's put away everything else. Think of it as me doing my job if it makes you feel better, but you need to rest. You can't keep going like this. You're no good to yourself, no good to Hannah if you're toast."

She pressed her lips together as if she was holding in something she wanted to say. He could imagine what that might be—that the last person she wanted to accept help from was him. Or something much worse. He'd certainly heard that before.

But she didn't say anything. She just stood, grabbed her bag and headed for the bathroom.

He stared at the closed door for several seconds before he returned his attention to Hannah. "You've got to promise me something, okay?" He doubted she understood him, but she at least seemed to be paying attention. "We've got to be quiet so your aunt Keri can get some sleep." As if she somehow had understood, she curled onto her side with the bunny in her arms.

Simon smiled at her. "You're going to be a heartbreaker someday. Keri will have to tote a shotgun to keep the boys away from you." Boys like he'd been.

He scrounged in the diaper bag and found a freshly made bottle, then scooped Hannah into his arms. He'd kill for a recliner right now, but the uncomfortable-looking chair at the table would have to do. He pulled it into the corner next to the door and sat with Hannah in his arms.

When Keri came out of the bathroom sporting loose gray pajama pants and a red Oktoberfest T-shirt, she stopped and looked at him. "Give her here. She can go to bed with me."

He shook his head. "She's not sleepy yet. We're just going to sit over here and get to know each other a little better."

Keri propped her hands on her hips. "And how am I supposed to sleep with you two engaging in baby talk in the corner?"

He met her stare. "Trust me, you're going to be out in less than five minutes."

If the situation had been any different, he would have laughed at the familiar fight he saw swirling just beyond the surface. Instead, she threw up her hands in an "I give up" gesture and headed for the bed. Once she'd curled beneath the comforter, she turned off the light next to the bed, leaving only the bathroom light to illuminate the room.

He glanced at the clock as Hannah continued to talk in baby language to her bunny. He'd overestimated how long it would take Keri to fall asleep. Two minutes after her head hit the pillow, she succumbed to fatigue.

That's when his own hit him. He slid down farther in the chair and pulled Hannah against his chest, banking on the bottle, quiet and lowered lighting putting her out, too. Once she was deeply asleep, he'd ease her into bed next to Keri and make his way to his own bed for some much-needed z's.

Hannah stilled, and the only sound was that of her sucking on her bottle. Eventually, even that stopped.

Somewhere in his mind, Simon realized he'd closed his own eyes and was perilously close to sleep. He had to get up. Maybe he could rest just another minute.

Chapter Three

Keri woke disoriented, unsure where she was. The bed didn't feel right, too hard with sheets not cool and smooth like her own. She blinked at the light filtering into the room. What the heck? She didn't sleep with lights on, not even a nightlight.

With another blink, reality slammed into her and tears sprang to her eyes. Sammi was gone.

She squeezed her eyes shut against the tears and the memories of the past couple of days. Simon delivering the news, the stressful drive to Dallas, the huge pit in her stomach as she'd met with a blurry cast of police, court and Child Protective Services representatives, and funeral officials. Then the hours of trying to get Hannah to stop crying.

Hannah.

She sat up and spotted her niece across the room, curled up and sleeping in Simon Teague's arms. She didn't know whether to be thankful or annoyed. By the sound of his breathing, he'd gone to sleep, too. Though how he could sleep with his big frame in that atrocious chair, she had no idea. Normally, she would love the idea of him being knotted into kinks when he woke up, but she couldn't muster her normal animosity toward him. Especially when he held Hannah so firmly and safely, ensuring she wouldn't tumble onto the floor.

She took the opportunity to really look at him, those long legs and strong arms, the handsome face with angular lines, the blond hair that was always lighter in the summer but now had darkened to its winter color that was more like straw. She'd never thought a man holding a baby could be sexy, but he somehow managed to pull it off.

Or maybe despite everything, she had to admit that there was a good reason Sheriff Simon Teague could charm any woman from the grandmothers manning the Hospital Auxiliary booth at Blue Falls Hospital to her niece. He was sexy as hell.

She had to get him out of her room before she forgot that he wasn't her favorite person. That he was the one who'd let Carter ruin his life.

Focusing on that old anger, she slid from the bed and strode quietly over to where he sat. As she reached for Hannah, his eyes opened.

"Is something wrong?" he asked, sounding way too concerned for her liking.

"I need to take her before you drop her."

He glanced down at Hannah snuggled against him, her little chest rising and falling in contented sleep. For the briefest, craziest moment, Keri envied her niece.

Instead of handing Hannah over, he pulled his legs beneath him and stood, careful not to jostle Hannah too much. "You want her in the bed or the carrier?"

She gave up trying to extricate her niece from him. "The bed." She flicked back the covers and watched as he eased Hannah onto the bed. Thankfully, she didn't wake up. Rather, she curled onto her side and hugged the bunny close.

Though she risked waking Hannah, Keri couldn't resist

dropping a kiss onto her baby-soft cheek as she tucked the covers around her. When she turned away from the bed, Simon was rotating and stretching his arms.

"They go to sleep?"

"Yeah, got the pins and needles thing going."

Why was she engaging him in conversation? She wanted him out of the room, out of Dallas, back out of her life.

And yet, she wasn't so blind and callous not to recognize what he'd done for her. She'd gotten some much-needed sleep all because he was willing to help and be uncomfortable, not something he had to do. It didn't make everything okay between them, but she was one to give credit where credit was due.

"Thank you," she managed, something she couldn't have imagined saying to Simon again only two days ago.

"No problem. She's a sweet kid." He looked as if he wanted to say something else, but instead he shifted and headed toward the door. "See you in the morning."

She nodded and followed him. This time, she didn't shut the door behind him quite so quickly. If pressed, she'd say it was because she didn't want to risk waking Hannah. Under no circumstances would she admit that his actions in the past twenty-four hours had softened her view of him.

One day of helpfulness didn't make up for not telling the truth when it mattered most.

SIMON HAD TO ADMIT IT was way better waking up in a bed than a crappy chair, even if the bed wasn't his own. The kinks he'd felt after holding Hannah for hours were gone, but he'd have no problem sleeping for another couple of days.

He lay staring at the ceiling and listening. No crying. He wondered if Keri and Hannah were still sleeping or had headed down to the lobby before the complimentary breakfast was over. At that thought, his stomach growled. He'd managed to eat a few bites of his barbecue dinner while he waited for Hannah to get tired but had left the rest behind in Keri's room when he'd retired to his own. Maybe he could nuke the rest of the sandwich.

Unwilling to get up quite yet, he reached for his cell phone on the nightstand and dialed his office.

"Sheriff's Department," Connor Murphy, one of his deputies, said on the other end of the line.

"It's me. How's it going down there?"

"Fine. Snow's pretty much all gone now. How's Keri?"

"Been better." Though she was holding up better than a lot of people would. But then she'd always been a tough cookie. He remembered how Clark Furst had teased her when she'd started developing breasts and how he'd gotten her fist to his jaw as a result. Sammi had been an athlete, too, but she'd had more feminine tendencies than Keri.

He closed his eyes and rubbed his calloused hand over his face. Still didn't seem real that Sammi was dead.

"You headed back today?" Connor asked.

"Not sure yet." Depended on when the funeral was. If it was quick, there was no point in driving back to Blue Falls only to have to turn around. "I'll call in later once I know more. Listen, I need you to run some checks for me. Try to locate Keri's brother. If I know Carter, there will be a ticket or arrest somewhere that'll point us in the right direction."

"Will do. I'll let you know when I find something."

Once Simon hung up, he dragged himself to the edge of the bed and stretched his back and shoulders. That's when he noticed the sheet of paper tucked under the door. Thinking it was the hotel bill, he retrieved it. But it wasn't a computer printout. He opened the piece of hotel stationery.

Sunshine came to pick us up early this morning.
Thanks for your help.
Keri.

He knew she was going through a horrible time, but something about the note made him angry. He stared at her writing and it hit him. She couldn't get away from him fast enough. Even after all these years, she still couldn't forgive him.

Well, that was partly his fault, wasn't it? She thought he hadn't told the truth in the aftermath of Carter's first arrest, and he hadn't. Only her idea of the truth and what had really happened weren't the same thing. Not that it mattered anymore.

He crumpled the paper into a tight ball and tossed it across the room into the trash can.

He'd done his duty. If he were smart, he'd just head home.

But then he wasn't the Teague brother most accused of being smart, was he?

SHE SHOULDN'T HAVE BROUGHT Hannah. As Keri sat in the front pew two days later, staring at the open caskets of her sister and brother-in-law, she kept hoping Hannah wouldn't notice her parents. She didn't want her to have nightmares, not like the ones Keri feared she'd have after this dreadfully long day was over.

Hannah still clung to the bunny Simon had given her, despite the fact Keri had bought her half a dozen other new toys. Keri tried not to be irritated, especially since the bunny was keeping her niece occupied as she sat on Keri's lap.

The sounds of the sermon and accompanying songs barely registered. She couldn't seem to focus on anything other than the sound of Ben's mother crying in the next pew over. Keri fought against her own tears, afraid they'd make Hannah cry, too. And right now, she couldn't handle another hours-long wailing session like the one they'd gone through at the hotel.

Simon had been her savior then, but she didn't want him to come to the rescue again. Didn't want him doing things that might tempt her to let go of her bitterness toward him. She needed something in her life to stay the same.

He'd shown up here. She'd seen him as she'd carried Hannah in through the lobby. Their eyes had only met for an instant, and she hated the way she felt guilty for running out on him at the hotel. There was no reason to feel guilty. She'd left him a note, after all.

Truth was, right now he wasn't the one she was mad at. Carter should be here with her, helping shoulder the burden of the sorrow and sudden responsibility for another human being. After Simon had asked her about him, she'd tried his number half a dozen more times as if she could magically make it be not disconnected anymore. The last time she'd had to restrain herself from throwing her cell phone against the wall.

Sunshine must have sensed her agitation because she reached over and clasped her hand. Keri squeezed back, thankful for her friend's strength beside her. They'd been friends almost from the moment Sunshine had walked into the bakery three years before and proclaimed she could make the best cinnamon rolls in Texas. She hadn't been wrong.

The rest of the funeral passed at the rate of a gla-
cier's advance. When it was time to sing the last hymn,
Keri stood on shaky legs. Hannah squirmed in her arms,
threatening to make Keri teeter off balance on her heels.

"Shh, honey," she whispered in the little girl's ear.
Thankfully, Hannah complied.

Somehow she held herself together as the parade of
mourners passed by and offered their condolences. Several felt the need to pat Hannah's back or smooth her hair.
She grew fidgety from all the attention, no doubt mostly
from people she didn't know. Keri was on the verge of
whisking her from the room when Sunshine extended her
arms.

"Let me take her."

Keri clasped Hannah closer for a moment, afraid of
letting Hannah out of her sight.

"We'll just be out in the lobby."

Hannah had been around Sunshine a lot the past couple
of days and occasionally before that when Sammi had
brought her to Blue Falls for visits. So she went to the
other woman without any fuss, especially when her eyes
lit on Brett, Sunshine's sixteen-year-old son. She'd glom-
med onto him like she had Simon. Already a little flirt
at ten months old. Brett took it all in stride and gave her
loads of attention.

Keri placed a tender kiss atop Hannah's head before
Sunshine carried her toward the lobby.

She turned slowly back toward the front of the room,
just in time to see Simon step away from Sammi's coffin.
No hint of his normal carefree self was visible. In fact, his
eyes were suspiciously bright. He had been friends with
Sammi, after all. She didn't have it in her to be cold to
him today.

His gaze met hers and he hesitated for the briefest

moment before walking her way. He didn't touch her like so many others had. "I'm sorry for your loss," he said instead.

He sounded so detached, so official, like a cop in a police drama on TV. A surge of anger rose in her until she realized this was likely how he coped with these types of situations. In his position as sheriff, he'd no doubt had to tell lots of families about the deaths of loved ones. How did he do it? Why would he want to be in the position to have to?

"Thanks." She lowered her gaze and noticed the suit he was wearing. Black and well cut. If this were any other day, she might have turned and admired how he looked in it from behind as he walked away. But it wasn't any other day. Plus, she still had more people waiting to express their condolences. Across the aisle, the Spencers were in the same boat.

Turned out Simon wasn't the only Teague in attendance. The whole clan filed by in a flurry of hugs and kind words. She held her breath, just trying to get through it all. It wasn't until Merline Teague, Simon's mom, stepped up to her that she felt she might finally lose the battle against her tears. Merline had this kind way about her that made everyone feel as if she was their second mom.

Though she'd dreaded all the touches all day, Keri suddenly needed a hug more than she needed her next breath. Merline opened her arms and Keri stepped into them.

"I'm so sorry, sweetie," Merline said. "If you need anything, don't hesitate to ask, okay?"

Keri nodded against Merline's shoulder, remembering how the older woman had said something very similar when Keri's mom had died. Keri had never held what

Simon did against his mother because Merline was a gem of a friend, neighbor and loyal customer.

When Keri stepped back, Merline held her hands a bit longer. "I know you are a very independent young woman, but we all need help sometimes. It's not a sign of weakness. Just keep that in mind."

Keri nodded because that was all she could manage without sobbing. Merline offered her a sympathetic smile that somehow gave her the strength she'd been searching for all day. After Merline took her leave, Keri only had to speak to a couple more mourners until she and the Spencers were the only people left in the room. Even the funeral home staff had stepped out to give them time to say their final goodbyes.

She sank onto the pew and examined her chewed nails and torn cuticles as the Spencers walked forward toward Ben's coffin. Keri couldn't approach Sammi's yet, not when anyone else was here to watch her. She had to be alone with her sister, one last time.

Holding in the burning need to sob uncontrollably was the hardest thing she'd ever done, made harder by the sounds of Ben's parents' grief. Just when she thought they might never leave, she detected movement. Still, she didn't look up, couldn't meet their eyes. The Spencers must have sensed that because they didn't stop next to her. Ben's dad squeezed her on the shoulder as they passed, leaving her alone to do what had to be done.

Keri didn't know how long she sat in the pew unable to move. Only the thought of the Spencers waiting to bury their son prompted her to stand, though the few steps it took to reach Sammi's coffin stretched out like miles. When she looked down at her sister, she couldn't decide if Sammi looked peaceful or as fake as a mannequin. Didn't matter. However she looked, this was all that was left of Samantha Jane Mehler Spencer.

Keri's chin trembled and tears finally spilled from her eyes. "Why did you have to leave?"

She wanted to be able to hug her sister one last time, to tell her how much she loved her. But she couldn't bring herself to touch the shell that had once been Sammi. She didn't want to know how cold and lifeless it was. She wanted to remember how warm and full of life her sister had been, how much she'd loved being a wife and mother.

With a trembling hand, Keri reached into the pocket of her jacket and pulled out a locket that held photos of their parents. She tucked it into the nook beneath Sammi's crossed hands, careful not to touch her.

"Here's Mom and Dad to keep you company until you can find them." So many tears flowed now that she could barely see her sister's face. Unwilling to appear sad and weepy in front of Hannah, she turned toward Ben for a moment and wiped away the evidence of her grief. "You take care of her, okay?" It might look crazy, talking to two people who were no longer there, but she needed to say the words, to make herself feel as if she still had some control, some power over how things should turn out. And as much as Ben had loved her sister in life, she had no doubt he'd be right by her side in the afterlife.

She took a deep, slow breath and turned back to Sammi. Gripping the edge of the coffin to keep herself upright, she took her last look at the sister she'd played with, fought with, competed against and emulated.

"I'll take good care of Hannah, I promise." She hesitated, knowing she had to leave but desperately hating the finality of it. With another deep breath, she released her hold on the coffin. "Goodbye, Sammi."

She turned and headed down the center aisle. Despite all the people waiting for her in the lobby, she'd never felt more alone.

FOR A WEEK, SIMON KEPT his distance. Instead of allowing himself to walk into the Mehlerhaus Bakery on the pretense of buying a slice of coffee cake, he kept to the opposite side of Main Street. Keri had made her feelings toward him clear with that note under the door. She'd accepted his help only because she hadn't had a choice.

Now she was back home where her friends could lend a hand and he could go back to being persona non grata.

Still, he wished he could bring her news of Carter. But other than one there-and-back border crossing to Mexico, he'd come up blank so far.

Despite the fact the falling out between Keri and Simon was partially his fault, it still bothered him. Today more so than it had a week ago. Truth was, he was tired of that wall between him and someone who'd once been his friend. As a general rule, he got along with people. Keri's obvious dislike for him was a burr that just kept digging deeper into his skin.

He replayed how she'd looked the day of the funeral, empty and alone. And he'd unexpectedly wanted to make that loneliness go away.

He didn't realize he'd stopped on the sidewalk and was staring at the bakery until Justine Ware stepped out of her real estate office behind him.

"How's she doing?" she asked as she nodded toward the bakery.

"Don't know. Haven't seen her since the funeral."

Justine hugged herself against the chill. "It's just so sad. I can't believe Sammi is gone."

He made a sound of agreement.

"I haven't gone over there since she came back," Justine continued. "Don't know what to say."

"Not much you can say. Just something she has to get through."

Justine's cell rang, prompting her to pull it from her pants pocket. "Sorry, need to take this. Business is slow this time of year, so I pounce on every opportunity I get."

He nodded as she hurried back inside saying, "Blue Falls Realty" into the phone.

He should head on to work, but he kept standing there watching as the morning crowd went in and out of the bakery's front door. He really would like a piece of coffee cake. Keri made the best cake of any type in town, though he only ever got a piece when someone brought it into the office. As he entered the crosswalk, he told himself he'd order his cake and a cup of coffee, blend into the crowd, take a quick glance to see how she was doing. Then he'd be off to his day of dealing with law and order.

The moment he stepped into the bakery, he inhaled the heavenly scents of baking bread and wafts of cinnamon. Looked like the rest of the crowd was enjoying its yeasty contact high, as well.

Sunshine was pulling a tray of bread loaves from the oven in the back while Keri handled the in-store crowd's orders and the phone. The bakery was always busy in the morning, but this crowd seemed extra large. He wondered if the colder weather had everyone craving hot coffee and carbs, or if the residents of Blue Falls were turning out in force to give Keri extra business as a means of condolence. As Justine said, what could you say in this type of situation? Maybe it was as simple as "I'd like a cinnamon roll and a large cup of coffee."

It all gave him a warm feeling until he saw Jo Baker, queen of the local gossips. His jaw tensed as Jo craned her neck to see beyond the people in front of her, no doubt hungry for a look at Keri, more interested in a morsel of gossip than a pastry. He tensed when it was Jo's turn at the counter.

"What can I get you?" Keri asked, a bit more clipped than usual.

"Oh, I don't know." Jo made a show of examining the offerings in the glass-fronted display case. "How are you doing? So sorry about your sister. Where's that sweet little girl? I'd love to see how much she's grown."

Simon resisted the urge to throttle the woman. "Come on, Jolene," he said, using her full name because he knew how much she hated it. "Some of us are hungry."

Keri's gaze lifted to his, and for the briefest moment he thought he saw gratitude there.

Jo placed her order, gave Keri her money and strode toward the door, giving him a squinty-eyed glare in the process.

As he moved up another spot in line, he heard Hannah start crying somewhere in the back. Keri looked over her shoulder caught between the throng of customers and her unhappy niece. Before he really thought about what he was doing, he headed for the room that served as Keri's office.

Hannah stood on shaky legs gripping the side of a playpen, her face red and streaked with tears.

"Hey there," he said as he crossed the small space. "What's all this fussing for?" He bent over and playfully poked her nose.

She sucked in a breath then paused, unsure whether to keep crying now that someone was paying her some attention. When she looked as if she might start crying again, he reached into the playpen and lifted her high in the air. "Now there, no more crying. You're too pretty to be scrunching your face up like that." He wiggled her in the air, causing her to giggle. He smiled at the sound, surprised how much he liked it.

He'd missed out on his nephew, Evan, at this age, but he was so going to spoil his new niece rotten.

Sunshine popped her head into the office. "Thank you. It's been nuts all morning."

"No problem. Hannah and I are already best buds, aren't we?"

Hannah picked at the top button on his shirt, and he wondered why it seemed to fascinate her.

Sunshine disappeared when the phone rang again, and he seated himself in the cushy chair across from Keri's desk.

"So, how's your day going?" he asked.

Hannah paused and gave him a grin that revealed a few tiny teeth.

"Are you flirting with me?"

As if she understood, Hannah giggled again.

He found a copy of *The Poky Little Puppy* on the desk, a copy that looked old enough to have been Keri's when she was little. After he read the book to Hannah, he placed her on his knee, one of her little legs on each side.

"So, you want to be a cowgirl? If so, you're going to have to learn how to ride a horse." He began bouncing his leg as he held her firmly at the waist. She laughed as if it was the funniest thing she'd ever experienced.

After a couple of minutes, he noticed Keri standing in the doorway.

"Look, Hannah, it's your aunt Keri." He changed his voice to a higher pitch. "Look, Aunt Keri. I'm a cowgirl."

A hint of a smile tugged at the edges of Keri's mouth and he found himself willing it to spread, to smooth away the lines of fatigue and sorrow. Then, as if she realized what she'd done, her lips formed a humorless line.

"Why are you doing this?" she asked.

He considered his answer for a moment before speaking. But then the truth made itself as clear as water. "Because once upon a time we were friends, and I'd like to be again."

He braced himself for a hot and sharp response, something about that ship having sailed, but it didn't come. Keri simply stood in the doorway for a few seconds, then turned to head back to work.

He wasn't about to examine why, but her response made him smile. Despite what he'd told her, he couldn't really explain this need to help her. Sure, they'd been friends before and the whole deal with Carter was long past due for resolution. But something deep inside told him those weren't the only reasons he was determined to place himself back in Keri Mehler's life.

He feared it might have a bit more to do with her long, slim body and chocolate-brown eyes. He was attracted to her, and no one was more surprised than him.

"So, what do you think, Hannah? Think I have a shot?"

Hannah smiled wide again, and he took that as a good sign.

Chapter Four

Keri looked up from replenishing the selection of fruit-filled pastries in the display case and wiped sweat from her forehead. She couldn't remember the last time the bakery had been so busy, but she was thankful for the nonstop pace of the past couple of hours. It kept her from thinking.

"Okay, I'm headed that way," Simon said into his hand-held radio as he strode through the kitchen.

Judging by the distinct lack of wailing coming from her office, he'd saved her once again. She shook her head, wondering how long it was going to take for her to figure out how to juggle work and caring for Hannah. She couldn't depend on Simon or anyone else to always be there to lend a hand. Sammi and Ben had left Hannah to her, and only her. Plus, Simon would no doubt wake up one day and remember they weren't friends anymore.

He paused once he reached the other side of the display case and wiggled his radio. "Duty calls."

"Anything wrong?"

"Harvey Turpin is off his meds again, waving a gun around. He's never shot anyone before, but there's a first time for everything."

Poor Harvey. He was a nice guy, wrote entertaining slice-of-life pieces for the local paper. But he didn't like to take the medication prescribed for his wild mood swings, convinced that he was better and didn't need them.

Simon nodded toward her office. "She's almost asleep."

"Thank you, again."

"Give me one of those crullers and we'll call it even."

She couldn't help but smile. It felt foreign after the past few days, but it felt so good, better than she wanted to admit. Like the boulder permanently sitting atop her chest had lightened a fraction.

When she handed Simon the pastry, his gaze caught hers for a moment. She wasn't sure what she saw there, but she couldn't look away. He really did have beautiful eyes.

"Be careful," she said, suddenly not liking the idea of him being around an unstable guy with a gun.

Something about what she'd said made him smile before he said, "Always," and headed out the door. She stared after him for a few seconds, breathless. When was the last time Simon had smiled at her?

Before the fiasco with Carter.

Despite her girlhood crush on him, his smile had never stunned her before. And it shouldn't now, she told herself as she closed the display case.

Getting the feeling that Sunshine was watching her a touch too closely, Keri grabbed the stack of orders below the phone hanging on the wall. "Looks like the holiday season has officially started."

"Yeah. Seems to begin earlier every year."

Which was good. It meant demand for the bakery's mail-order products was increasing. Keri had been working toward that goal ever since she'd assumed the helm of Mehlerhaus. But now she had mixed feelings. On the one hand, the extra income would be useful. On the other hand, she now had a child to raise.

She blinked back tears, forbidding herself to think about Sammi now. Not when she had work up to her eyeballs and hours before she could go home and collapse.

As she flipped through the orders, she wasn't able to keep herself from thinking about the other side of things. That more orders also meant more demands on her time. Right when she needed to devote it to Hannah.

"Don't worry," Sunshine said as she started slicing a pumpkin cake. "We'll get through it."

Keri suspected her friend meant more than the busy season.

As Hannah started crying again, she wasn't so sure.

HE'D DONE SOME PRETTY dumb things in his time on Earth, but entertaining the idea of making a play for Keri Mehler ranked right up there. Especially now. What kind of lowlife made a move on a woman when she was grieving? Plus, chances were that when she'd had time to adjust to her new reality, she'd go back to ranking him right between slugs and fungus.

He'd already helped her more than either of them could have ever expected. The best thing he could do for her now was to stay away and keep from reminding her of painful losses.

But he'd continue digging around, trying to find Carter for her. Her brother should be here, helping her. No matter what he'd done or where he'd gone, Carter should know about Sammi.

As Simon pulled into Harvey's driveway, he shifted his thoughts away from Keri and her MIA brother. When he saw Harvey gesturing wildly with a .357, it brought home that now wasn't the smartest time to be distracted. He parked next to a sprawling live oak behind Jack Fritz's patrol car and got out very carefully. The last thing he wanted to do was spook Harvey into ventilating anyone, including himself.

"What's got his knickers in a bunch today?" Simon asked the older deputy.

"You name it— Cowboys losing, politics, price of beer. Pretty much your typical 'the world's going to hell in a handbasket' tirade."

Simon eyed Harvey where he now sat atop his front steps, ranting about every politician in Austin being a crook.

"You know, I really like Harvey when he's behaving and taking his meds," Simon said. "Not so much when he doesn't and becomes a cantankerous old goat."

"Our very own Jekyll and Hyde."

"This was not the day to not have my full supply of morning coffee." Simon sighed. "Well, might as well get on with the disarming or the shooting."

Jack grunted. "I'm getting too old for this garbage."

"Have medical on standby."

"Already called them. They're waiting at the end of Rattlesnake Road."

Simon eased out from behind the car, unsnapping his holster as he moved, and edged slowly up the gentle slope toward the house. "Hey, Harvey. How's it going?"

"Who's that?"

"Now, Harvey, you're going to hurt my feelings. You've known me since I was born."

"Simon?"

"Got it in one."

"What are you doing out here?"

"Came to ask why you're sitting out here in the cold waving that .357 around. I know there aren't any rattlesnakes out today."

"There's snakes aplenty. They just have two legs."

"Well, I can't argue with that. Hope you don't include me in that category."

Harvey seemed to think about that for a moment longer than Simon would have liked, and he resisted the urge to place his palm atop his sidearm.

"Nah, you're a good sort," Harvey finally said, allowing Simon to breathe a smidge easier.

"You are, too, Harvey. But you do tend to make people nervous when you're waving a gun around."

Harvey looked at the gun in his hand as if he couldn't for the life of him figure out why it was there.

"How about you set that gun down and we'll talk about what's bothering you?"

Harvey lowered the gun, then hesitated, twisting it in his hand to examine it, before placing it on the porch beside his right hip. "Ah, hell, I'm in trouble again, aren't I?"

"You haven't hurt anyone, and you're on your own property, but I do need you to go to the hospital and get your medication back in order."

Harvey grimaced. "That stuff makes me feel like I've got cotton for brains."

"I'm sorry about that, but it keeps you from scaring the neighbors and maybe hurting someone. You don't want to hurt anyone, do you?"

Harvey sighed, then shook his head.

Simon slowly edged closer until he was able to remove Harvey's gun from his side. He made a sign to Jack to call in the ambulance.

After all the ranting, Harvey had gone quiet. He stared at the ground, probably trying to straighten out the spaghetti-like jumble of his thoughts. Simon couldn't imagine what it must be like to have to take pills to keep his brain functioning properly. Honestly, maybe he did need some pharmaceutical aid after the ride his thoughts had taken on the crazy train that morning.

Harvey ran his hands over his face, and Simon couldn't help but feel sorry for the guy. He'd always been a touch moody, but when he'd lost his wife, Melissa, ten years before because of a staph infection after minor surgery, he'd gotten a lot worse. Simon didn't know why he hadn't realized it before, but maybe Harvey was just lonely. Maybe he didn't refuse to take his medicine because he thought he'd be okay without it. Perhaps he didn't take it so he could forget.

Simon watched as the ambulance pulled up, ready to have this call done and over with. Seemed like he was encountering sadness at every turn, and it was making him uncomfortable. Maybe after work he'd stop by the Frothy Stein for a beer.

By the time he got through the rest of the day, he really needed that drink. From Harvey's, he'd gone to a wreck scene—car versus cattle hauler. Luckily, no one was seriously hurt. Add to that a domestic disturbance, cattle loose out on Austin Highway and eighty-year-old Bernice Watson taking her walking cane to the neighbor's dog after it bit her, and he was wondering why he'd decided not to work at his family's guest ranch full-time like his brothers.

When he walked out of the sheriff's department, he noticed the air had warmed a few degrees. Hey, at least one positive out of the day.

The memory of the gratitude in Keri's eyes came back to him. Maybe she was warming to him, mimicking the change in the weather. He glanced down the street toward the bakery, considering checking in on her.

What are you playing at, fool?

He'd never thought of Keri as anything more than a

friend. Why was he suddenly noticing her curves and the soft look of her lips? Couldn't be the vulnerable thing—he'd never gone for that type.

But that was just it. As a rule, Keri Mehler wasn't vulnerable, no matter what she went through. In fact, she was one of the strongest—and most stubborn—women he knew. Maybe that's why seeing her so sad and overwhelmed didn't sit well with him.

He was halfway to the bakery before he stopped and reconsidered. Did he really want to put himself in her line of fire when she snapped back to normalcy and realized the enemy had invaded her camp?

Before he stepped too far into her life, he changed course. Maybe someday they could be friends again, but now wasn't the time.

"Evening, Sheriff," said Lou Maples, the Stein's owner, as Simon parked himself at the bar.

"Lou."

"You look like you've had a long day."

"Long week."

Damn thing had felt more like a year.

He'd only consumed half his beer when a ruckus started in the corner by the pool tables. He turned on his stool just in time to hear Adam Parker insult T. J. Malpin's manhood then get a pool cue over the head for his trouble.

"You have got to be kidding me," Simon mumbled.

He should have gone to the bakery.

No, he should have gone home. Which was where he was headed as soon as he did some ass kicking of his own.

KERI PAUSED IN THE MIDST of boxing up an order of lemon tarts to stifle a yawn. Her bed called to her, but she still had several things she wanted to finish before going home. Thankfully, Hannah seemed to be in a better mood after a long nap. Amazing how a set of car keys and an empty box could provide hours of entertainment.

She was just closing the last box of tarts for a wedding reception the next evening when the front door opened with probably the last customer of the night.

"Know where a guy can get a cup of strong coffee?"

She started in surprise at the sound of Simon's voice, despite the fact he'd been a familiar fixture the past few days. She was too tired to figure out how she felt about that. Fact was it took energy she didn't have to stay mad at him. Didn't mean she liked him, though.

Keri fastened the pastry box and turned toward him. And gasped. His lip was busted and swelling, and it looked as if his right eye might have tangled with a fist or two.

"Looks like you need more than a cup of coffee."

"If you're hiring, I might be in the market for a new job."

She snorted at the idea of Simon kneading dough or crafting fondant. "Going to trade your Stetson for a chef's hat, are you?"

"If the doughnuts don't punch back."

She poured him the cup of coffee and passed it over the counter. He tried to pay her, but she waved away his cash.

"Let me pay you."

She hesitated, mentally stumbling over her unusual gratitude toward him. "No, you've helped me a lot in the past week."

"It was nothing. Besides, you already gave me a cruller."

"I don't think that's quite enough."

He smiled, though he winced at how it pulled at his split lip. "It was a really good cruller."

She found herself rolling her eyes at him the way she'd done so many times years ago. That thought dimmed her faint flicker of a better mood.

"So, Harvey do that?" she asked as she gestured toward his face. "Don't tell me you got beat up by a guy twenty years older than you."

"No, this is courtesy of a pool game that got a little out of hand at the Stein."

"And your face happened to get in the way."

"Something like that. But Adam Parker and T. J. Malpin will be spending the night as guests of the county, and I'll be sleeping in my own bed."

The image of him in bed spooked her so much she knew she was running on too little sleep. Why else would that brief image send warmth sluicing through her?

She shook her head as she shoved a scoop of ice into a plastic carryout bag. "I can't decide if those two are best friends or mortal enemies." As she rounded the front counter, she spotted him testing the tenderness in his jaw.

"Little of both," he said.

"C'mon, sit down," she said, doing her best to sound exasperated, and not think of him wearing next to nothing below soft sheets.

"I'm okay."

"Sit. Can't have you coming in here looking like you've gone twelve rounds with George Foreman. You'll scare off the customers."

He glanced at the clock on the wall. "It's past closing time."

"And yet here you are," she said as she slid into the chair next to him.

"So are you."

"I have work to do." She lifted the ice pack to his eye, and maybe she pressed it a touch too hard to remind herself that she didn't like him. Simon winced at the rough treatment and grunted. She shook her head again. "Didn't it occur to you to duck?"

"I did. The pool cue, anyway. T.J.'s fist was a different story."

She laughed just a little, surprised she remembered how. She ignored the sting of guilt. Laughter shouldn't be a part of her life just days after burying her sister. And yet when she looked at the man sitting in front of her, the urge was there. She hoped Sammi would forgive her.

"This reminds me of the time you got hit in the cheek by that baseball," she said. "Now, that was a shiner." She removed the ice and examined the skin around his eye. "Don't think this one will be as bad."

"Wouldn't know it by how it feels."

She tossed the ice pack on the table between them. "Quit being such a wimp."

"Wimp?"

"Yeah, wimp."

When he smiled at her again, she shoved to her aching feet. Why couldn't he just leave her alone so she could finish her work? So she could go home and sleep and wake up tomorrow free of insane thoughts about him. After all, this was the man who'd refused to tell the previous sheriff that Carter wasn't guilty of the vandalism that brought about his first arrest. The reason her brother wasn't here now helping her take care of his niece.

She retraced her steps and pulled the last of the day's cash from the register drawer. Once she prepared the night's deposit, she was going home to collapse.

"Can I help you with anything?" Simon asked from where he still sat icing his eye.

"No, I'm almost done." There were other things she could do, but they were going to wait until morning. Now she wanted to get away from Simon and how he was confusing her.

He seemed to take the hint and stood. "Thanks for the coffee and ice pack."

She nodded and made a sound of acknowledgment, but she didn't look at him. Out of the corner of her eye, she noticed him hesitate before tossing what was left of the ice pack and heading for the door.

"Good night, Keri."

"Good night." She did glance up then and was startled to see him watching her more closely than was comfortable.

He tapped the front of his hat and walked out into the night. She waited, not moving, until he was out of sight before she crossed to the door and locked it. As she kept herself upright by gripping the door handle, she wondered if she'd ever feel rested again. Would she ever feel normal?

She looked out the window in time to see Simon crossing the street to his SUV. Leaning her forehead against the cold glass of the door, she answered her own question. Nothing was ever going to feel normal again.

Sammi was gone.

Hannah was now her responsibility.

And Simon Teague was occupying way too many of her thoughts.

KERI HAD BEEN RIGHT ABOUT his eye. As Simon stared at his shiner the next morning, the black and blue didn't match the result of the baseball-to-the-eye incident. Still, didn't mean it was pretty.

He shook his head, trying to clear thoughts of Keri

and how she'd surprised him by nursing his eye the night before. He couldn't figure out why he suddenly felt this pull to be around her, but it was still plaguing him this morning.

Determined to stay away from the bakery today, he dressed and headed out to his family's ranch. Because of his post as sheriff, he'd taken an apartment a block from the office. But the Vista Hills Ranch still felt like home. Every other member of his family lived there. His parents in the main house where he'd grown up. Nathan, his wife, Grace, and their son, Evan, at the edge of the ranch. And Ryan and his new wife, Brooke, the ranch's cook and guest relations manager, in his small cabin not far from the main house.

Everyone helped in the running of the ranch in some way. And despite the fact he had a full-time job and lived in town, he did his part as well in helping with the upkeep of the ranch's buildings. Today, that meant fixing a leaky sink in one of the guest cabins and reattaching a gutter to another.

He met Grace heading out the ranch's entrance road as he drove in, no doubt on her way to work at her interior design studio in town. They waved as they passed, then he made the turn that led up to the guest cabins. Things were quieter around the ranch this time of year, but through Brooke's advertising efforts half the cabins were still full. When he pulled up in front of one of the empty ones, he sat staring at it for a moment. It hit him how much had changed on the ranch in the past several months. At this time last year, all three Teague sons had been living the bachelor life. Now, both of his younger brothers were married men and seemed very happy about that fact.

An unfamiliar and unexpected twinge centered itself

in his chest. How could he feel lonely when there were more people here than ever? Besides, he wasn't a lonely kind of guy. He, more so than Nathan and Ryan, embraced being single. The longest he'd been in a relationship was six months, and that was in high school.

Why did his carefree lifestyle suddenly seem less appealing than it had just a few days ago?

What the hell was he thinking? He needed to get himself a date and take a few turns around the dance floor at the music hall. Maybe Justine Ware was free tonight.

When Keri's face popped into his mind, he growled and got out of his truck. He grabbed his toolbox and headed inside the cabin.

Several minutes later when he'd finally contorted himself under the sink and found the problem, he heard the front door open.

"Simon?"

"In here, Mom."

"That looks comfortable," she said when she entered the kitchen.

"Yeah, I'm thinking of sleeping like this from now on." He tightened the slip nut at the joint between two pipes, then scooted his way back out. When he sat up, his mom's eyes widened.

"What on earth happened to you?" She crossed the room, reaching him as he stood.

"Had to break up a little disagreement at the Stein last night."

Merline Teague shook her head slowly. "Looks like you should have ducked."

"You sound like Keri." He realized his mistake as soon as the words left his mouth.

"You've talked to Keri?"

"I grabbed a cup of coffee there last night after tossing

the disagreeing parties behind bars." He tried to sound casual about it, though he doubted he was fooling his mom. She was about as sharp and observant as they came. Which had made getting away with mischief all but impossible when he and his brothers had been growing up.

"How is she doing?"

"Seemed fine, considering. Tired, I guess."

"That poor girl has been through more than any one person should have to go through in a lifetime."

He didn't say anything, but he totally agreed. Keri and he were the same age, and already she'd lost both parents as well as her only sister and brother-in-law. And her brother was out of the picture more often than not. He couldn't imagine losing any single member of his family, let alone nearly all of them.

"I wonder if we could put together a group of people to help her out, maybe babysit Hannah, clean house."

Simon tossed his wrench back into the toolbox. "Mom, do you really think Keri would allow that? You know how independent she is."

"Everyone needs help sometimes. Ryan wasn't much on accepting help, either, but Brooke changed his mind about that."

Uncomfortable with the direction in which the conversation was shifting, Simon turned his back to his mom and flipped the water on. After checking to make sure the drip was fixed, he started washing his hands.

"What happened between you two?" his mom asked.

It took him a moment to realize she meant their falling-out and not how he'd found himself strolling back into Keri's life. She'd never asked him before, and now he couldn't find a good reason not to tell her. He turned back toward her and leaned against the sink as he dried his hands with paper towels.

"You remember when Carter was arrested for spray painting Mrs. Abbott's house?"

"Yeah."

Suddenly, Simon felt like a stupid teenager again, anxious about telling the truth that would get him into a heap of trouble. He wasn't a boy anymore, but he still didn't relish the idea of his mom being disappointed in him.

"I was with him."

His mom's eyebrows bunched in confusion.

"I didn't take part, but I was with him when he did it. When I heard the police siren, I ran and left him there."

"But...I thought Sheriff Tyler just talked to you because you and Carter were friends."

"He did. Only Carter knew I was there, and he didn't say anything." A guilt that hadn't paid a visit in a long time hit him in the gut. "Keri thought Carter and I were together, just not at Mrs. Abbott's house. She got angry when she assumed I didn't tell the sheriff that he had the wrong person."

"You didn't ever tell her the truth?"

"She was convinced that if either of us had done it, it was me and Carter was taking the fall. I was mad at Mrs. Abbott for a bad grade, and Carter talked me into getting some spray paint and going over to her house. But I backed out. He didn't."

His mom shook her head. "But after all this time, and she still thinks you were the one who did it?"

"At the very least that I let Carter get arrested for something he didn't do. I never had the guts to admit I was even there. I didn't want you and Dad to find out."

It all sounded so pathetic now.

"And Carter never told Keri, either?"

He shook his head.

His mom crossed her arms, and he sensed a reprimand a long time in coming.

"You owe her the truth."

"What good is that going to do now? It'll just hurt her more." Better that she stay mad at him than to have one more thing taken away, the belief in her brother's innocence.

He found it difficult to meet his mother's eyes, afraid she'd see too much of what even he didn't understand.

"Lies are never the right path." His mom stepped toward him and placed her palm against his upper arm. "You and Keri were once good friends, and right now she needs friends more than ever."

He knew that, but what he was supposed to do with that knowledge he had no idea.

After his mom left, he stood in the quiet kitchen without moving, wondering if there was a snowball in hell's chance of him and Keri ever being friends again. Especially if he told her the truth.

Chapter Five

Keri had a tray of hot pastries in each hand and the phone was ringing off the hook when Simon stepped into the bakery two days after he'd come by for late-night coffee and an ice pack. Great, one more thing she had to deal with this morning. She was just getting a hint of her equilibrium back after their last encounter.

Without saying anything to him, she slid the hot trays onto the metal table in the center of the kitchen.

The phone stopped midring, just before Simon said, "Mehlerhaus Bakery."

She shifted her attention to the front of the building, where Simon stood with the phone pressed to his ear and a pen in the other. As she stood dumbfounded, he handled what sounded like a mail order, taking down all the pertinent details.

When he hung up, he ripped the piece of paper from the notepad and turned toward her. Holding up the paper, he said, "An order for two dozen molasses cookies."

It took her several seconds for words to coalesce in her brain. "Thanks. How'd you know what to ask?"

"I heard you and Sunshine taking orders the other day when I was here."

"Oh."

The phone rang again just as a couple stepped in the front door. Simon gestured toward the customers.

"I'll get the phone," he said.

By the time Keri had boxed up an assortment of pastries and a coffee cake for the older couple, who were in town to do some Christmas shopping, Simon had taken two more orders.

"Is it like this all the time?" he asked.

"Right after Halloween, things get really busy."

He scanned the kitchen. "Where's Sunshine?"

She rearranged what was left of the scones and shut the display case. "Out with the flu. Her whole family has it."

Worst possible timing.

"Do you hire seasonal help?"

"I've thought about it, but things are just…so unsure right now. I don't want to make any rash financial decisions." There was still Sammi and Ben's estate to finalize, and who knew what kind of bills might be outstanding. Plus, she had no idea how expensive it was going to be to raise Hannah. She'd nearly had a stroke in the middle of the H-E-B grocery the night before when she'd seen the price of diapers.

Simon braced his hand against the metal table that ran the length of the wall from the front counter to the ovens. "You can't do this all by yourself."

"I'll be fine." She hated how tired her voice sounded when she'd tried so hard to sound strong. Hated that he'd seen her weak at every turn lately.

"Simon—" Before she could finish, the chaos that was her life assaulted her from every side with the phone ringing, the front door admitting customers and Hannah crying from the playpen in Keri's office. For a moment, she wanted nothing more than to run out the back door and not look back.

She froze when Simon placed his hand on her shoulder. "Go on. I'll take care of things out here."

Though it made her a horrible person, she just couldn't face Hannah's crying right now.

"Or, how about I visit little Miss Hannah?"

She nodded, too ashamed to meet his eyes. Hard work in the bakery, she was used to. Doughnuts and cakes didn't look up at her with tears in their eyes wondering where their mother was, why this sorry excuse for a replacement couldn't manage to keep her happy.

Somehow she managed to pull herself together long enough to help a flurry of customers, take two phone orders, schedule a wedding cake consultation and accept a delivery of shipping boxes from Erik Thompson, the UPS guy.

When the bakery was empty and quiet, she heard Simon talking to Hannah. Part of her was annoyed that he could so easily calm Hannah, but another part was thankful. She should go to her niece, relieve Simon from babysitting duty, but her feet wouldn't move that direction.

Baking, she knew. Dealing with customers, ditto. But raising a baby? There she was as lost as if she'd been dumped in Russia and told to talk her way out. When she'd agreed to be Hannah's guardian, the thought that something might actually happen to Sammi hadn't even occurred to her. They'd already lost their parents too soon. Fate couldn't possibly be that cruel.

But it had.

She eyed the doorway into her office and felt the weight of responsibility press down on her.

Sammi, what were you thinking?

Simon waited for Keri to make an appearance at the office door to check on her niece, but she stayed away.

The longer she kept herself busy in the bakery, the more sure he became of what he'd seen in her eyes—distance. Of all the things vying for her attention, she'd least wanted to deal with Hannah.

God, how he hoped that was temporary. Hannah had lost everyone else. She didn't deserve to be with someone who didn't want her.

No, it had to be that Keri was still grieving and saw her sister every time she looked at Hannah. Because he'd seen her with Hannah before, and she'd doted on that little girl.

He glanced into the playpen where Hannah seemed satisfied with her assortment of toys.

"Now you behave, okay?" he said. "Time for me to go check on your aunt."

When he stepped out of the office, Keri was decorating a wedding cake.

"Who's getting married?" he asked.

She finished squeezing the icing out of whatever those tube things were called. "A couple over in Sisterdale." She glanced at the clock shaped like a pink-frosted cake. "Don't you have to go to work?"

"Not till this afternoon." As he took in the slump of her shoulders and the dark circles under her eyes, he made a split-second decision. "I'm yours for the morning."

Keri's eyes widened. "What?"

"You're a person short, so put me to work."

She shook her head. "Simon, I can manage."

He wasn't going to let her pull that independent crap with him today, shoving him away like she'd been trying to do since the night he'd come to tell her about Sammi's death. He crossed his arms and didn't budge from where he stood.

"Either you give me something to do, or I'm just going to make stuff up."

She exhaled and braced her weight against the metal prep table. "Why are you even here?"

He met and held her gaze. "Because I want to be."

A visible jolt went through her. She seemed as surprised and shaken by that simple truth as he was. He expected her to kick him out, but she only stared at him as if he was some complex puzzle. That was a first. He was about as uncomplicated as they came.

"Fine," she finally said. "That stack of orders by the phone needs to be put into the computer system."

He grabbed the pile of order slips. "Point the way."

As he followed her into the office, he noticed that she glanced at Hannah but didn't say anything to her. When Hannah spotted him, she smiled and held up her arms. Unable to resist, he leaned down to pick her up.

"We've got to stop meeting this way," he said as he placed her on his hip. "People will begin to talk."

"You're going to spoil her, and I can't pick her up every time she cries," Keri said.

There it was again, that distance. Was she even aware of it?

"I don't think a little attention will hurt her."

"And you're not the one who has to get up with her at night when she cries because she wants her mother and all she's got is me." Keri's lower lip trembled.

When he took a step toward her, she backed away and held up her hand, palm out.

"Let's just get this done. Please. I have a million other things to do."

He'd wanted to comfort her, but she wasn't ready for that. Plus, he was probably the last person on earth she'd accept any type of comfort from. And what did he know about helping anyone through grief, anyway? Usually, his involvement ended after he'd delivered the bad news. But he was unable to just walk away from Keri and the pain he knew in his gut she was trying to avoid by building a wall around herself. He'd seen it before—when her parents died, then again when Carter had left her all alone to keep up the family home and business.

Hannah started to fuss when he lowered her to the playpen, but she quieted when he turned on one of her toys that made music and had light-up shapes.

When he rounded the desk, he was careful to give Keri the room she needed. He watched as she walked him through the data entry process.

"Got it?" she asked when she finished and turned to face him.

"Yeah." He stepped back to let her pass him, but there wasn't much room and for a moment they stood so close he could smell her shampoo or lotion. Whichever it was, it smelled like peaches.

She paused for a moment to look at Hannah, and the longing on her face was painful to see. As if she remembered he was in the room, she looked away and hurried out the door.

For several minutes, he didn't get much done. He kept looking toward the doorway, fighting against an unexpected longing of his own. He couldn't believe how much he'd wanted to pull Keri into his arms and hold her, give her someone to lean on. Hold her close so he could inhale her scent more deeply.

He shook his head to rid himself of those crazy images, but it didn't work. Instead, he forced himself to keep his mind on the work at hand. Though his attention kept being drawn to the door every time Keri walked by, he finished entering the orders and headed out of the room for his next task.

Some of the tension between them ebbed as the morning progressed. Honestly, he was surprised by how well they worked together. Not that Keri was overly chatty, except with the customers. Sometimes he got the feeling she spoke with them as long as she did so she wouldn't have to speak to him. But together they managed to handle the customers popping in for something sweet, the phone calls and Hannah's needs.

When the bakery grew quiet later in the morning, he started helping her package orders for shipment without her asking.

"You've really increased the bakery's business, haven't you?" he asked as he fastened a box of spice cookies, then slapped on the mailing label.

She nodded as she prepared several orders with an efficiency that spoke of much practice. "It was slow at first, but it's picked up the past couple of years. Sometimes…" She paused and he watched as she swallowed hard. "Sometimes Sammi would even come down this time of year and help out."

As if she'd heard her mother's name and recognized it, Hannah cried out. Simon taped another box shut before stepping toward the office.

"Simon."

He met Keri's eyes and refused to look away. His words were going to hurt, but he felt in his gut that she needed to hear them. "She's not used to being alone, Keri."

She didn't say anything in response, just glanced toward the office and gave a small nod. That was a step in the right direction.

When he scooped Hannah out of the playpen, she gave one of those happy baby squeals. His heart constricted when he thought about how she was going to grow up not knowing her parents. Poor Sammi and Ben, unable to see their sweet little girl become a woman. Sometimes life was just damned unfair.

As he stepped back into the kitchen, Hannah got excited again and waved her little arms, bonking him on the head with a stuffed duck in the process.

"Hey, there. Keri, your niece is beating me with waterfowl."

Keri gave an unexpected snort of laughter, and that simple sound made him way happier than it should.

"She knows a scoundrel when she sees one." A hint of the girl Keri had once been, when she hadn't taken any guff from any of the boys, surfaced for a moment before she seemed to remember again that she shouldn't be happy.

He played at covering up Hannah's ears. "Don't listen to her. She's just jealous that you're the apple of my eye."

He hadn't meant to flirt with Keri, but it didn't feel wrong. In fact, it felt natural in a way. Maybe it was just because that's how he typically dealt with any female.

Or maybe not.

He had no doubt she'd heard him, but she ignored him and kept on working. While her attention was averted, he watched her. The way her long-sleeved T-shirt hugged her shape, a shape that hadn't yet made its full appearance when they'd stopped speaking to each other. How wisps of her dark hair escaped the knot on top of her head to frame her face. Her long, nimble fingers making quick work of her task. As she smoothed mailing labels on boxes, he wondered what those fingers would feel like gliding across his skin.

So lost was he in his imagination that he didn't immediately notice when she looked up and caught him staring.

"What's wrong?"

"Uh, nothing." He glanced at the clock.

Keri did the same. "You have to go?"

"In a few minutes." He shifted his attention in a safer direction, toward Hannah. With her resting on his hip, he walked toward the worktable and stood on the opposite side from Keri. "Enjoy being a baby while you can, Hannah. Before long, your aunt Keri will have you out here shipping cookies to Outer Mongolia."

Keri gave him a raised-eyebrow look. "Outer Mongolia, really? Not sure German baked goods are big there."

"They just haven't tasted your baking yet."

He'd swear he saw color flush her cheeks as she looked down at the order sheet on the table. That he could make her blush made him smile.

When the front door opened, Justine Ware walked in. Keri nearly bolted for the front counter, and he couldn't help but watch the way her body moved as she did so. In that moment, he wasn't thinking of Keri as a friend or an adversary. He was thinking of her as one hundred percent pure woman, and it shook him and warmed him at the same time.

"What can I get you?" Keri asked Justine.

He could think of a few things he'd like for her to get him.

Damn, he was losing his mind. Why was he suddenly imagining kissing Keri Mehler of all people?

Because she'd grown up to be very kissable.

With an inward groan, he headed toward the office to return Hannah to her playpen. He had to get out of the bakery, shift his thoughts in a different direction. For some reason, his feelings for Keri were getting all tangled up. And he wasn't a tangled feelings kind of guy. He was a casual dating with no strings kind of guy.

To remind himself of that fact, he headed straight for Justine after depositing Hannah back in the playpen.

"You moonlighting as a pastry chef now?" Justine asked when he rounded the front counter.

"Just lending a hand." He had to wipe that curious expression off Justine's face. "You free tonight?"

The question surprised her, and though he didn't look straight at Keri he got the feeling it had surprised her, too. But it shouldn't. This was who he was, and everyone knew it.

Then why did it not sit well with him today?

"Uh, yeah," Justine said. "After this house showing is over." She nodded at the tray of finger-size pastries she'd ordered for the open house.

"Great. Feel like going dancing?"

Justine glanced at Keri, but he pretended he didn't see it. "Sure," she said, a touch more hesitantly than he was used to when he asked a woman out.

"Good. I'll pick you up at seven." He hazarded a brief glance at Keri, but she was looking down. "Well, got to get to work."

Though he'd done nothing out of the ordinary, he nonetheless felt like a giant heel as he strode out the front door.

"WHAT WAS THAT ALL ABOUT?" Justine asked as she watched Simon head down the sidewalk.

A very good question.

Justine turned her attention back to Keri. With some wariness, she asked, "Are you two talking again?"

Keri shrugged. "In passing."

When Justine looked back into the kitchen, Keri could almost hear the questions zipping through the other woman's mind.

"Sunshine has the flu, so he helped out a bit this morning." What was she doing? She didn't have to explain. It wasn't as though Simon being in the bakery all morning was any big deal.

Obviously not if he'd asked out Justine right in front of her.

Not that that mattered, either. Getting involved with Simon Teague was the last thing on earth she wanted to do.

Then why had a jolt of jealousy gone through her when he'd asked Justine to go dancing?

No, that wasn't jealousy. It was annoyance, pure and simple. He might act like he was different, grown-up and responsible, but at his core Simon hadn't changed at all.

"Then you don't mind?"

Justine, who had been in the same grade as Sammi, looked hesitant when Keri met her gaze. "Mind what?"

"Me going out with Simon?"

"You've gone out with him before, haven't you?"

"Once, a few years ago. Nothing serious."

The idea that Justine might want something serious with Simon settled like an unwelcome guest in Keri's middle.

"I just thought maybe you two—"

"Me and Simon? Not in this lifetime." But she couldn't drum up the same level of disgust with him she once had.

"Okay, then. Well, I better get to this open house if I hope to sell something this month."

"Good luck," Keri said, trying to push away the stupid bitterness she felt toward someone she'd always considered a friend.

When Justine left, Keri poured herself a cup of coffee and got back to work. Though she really was thankful for the help Simon had given her that morning, she wished he'd never set foot back in the bakery. She'd been frazzled and overworked before he'd pitched in, but now that she'd gotten used to his presence in the kitchen she missed it. Every time the front door opened, a little hitch of anticipation rose in her chest even though she knew he was at work.

Why couldn't she stop thinking about him?

Maybe it was just because he was good with Hannah or how he'd helped her out lately. Or maybe, if she was honest with herself, it was those long legs encased in denim, his strong upper body and that sexy grin of his. Her skin flushed with heat. She felt like a teenager again, daydreaming about the best-looking boy in school, the one she couldn't tell how she felt because he was her brother's best friend.

No matter how hard she tried to push thoughts of Simon out of her mind for the rest of the day, it didn't work for very long. Finally, exhausted from trying, she sank into the comfortable old chair opposite her office desk. Hannah lay on her tummy in the middle of the playpen taking a nap, the bunny Simon had given her hugged close. She watched as Hannah's back slowly rose and fell in the rhythm of sleep. Keri ached to hold her as close as Hannah was holding that bunny, but an unspeakable fear assaulted her every time she considered it. She loved that child with all her heart, and that's what scared her. Every time she loved someone, they left her.

Once again, her thoughts strayed to Simon. She closed her eyes and shook her head. She didn't love Simon, hadn't even liked him in a very long time. He'd never been hers to lose.

But she had lost him, hadn't she? When he'd let her brother take the rap for something he didn't do, Simon had sealed his fate.

She had to believe the only reason he was waltzing past her defenses now was because she was so incredibly tired.

The sound of the front door opening jolted her awake. Disoriented, it took her a few seconds to fully pull herself from the depths of sleep. Footsteps coming closer made her jump to her feet and head toward the office door. When she reached it, she nearly ran into Simon. He reached out and steadied her.

"Are you okay?"

He wore jeans and a black button-up shirt, and black boots. And the smell of him, a mixture of woodsy soap, heat and something indefinable but very, very male, made every female part of her stand up and take notice.

She also noticed that it was dark outside.

"Keri?" he said.

She blinked and pulled herself out of his grasp. "I'm fine. What are you doing here? I thought you were burning up the dance floor tonight."

"Justine had to cancel."

She did? Keri reined in the crazy surge of happiness that news brought with it. Irritated at herself, she tried to push past Simon into the kitchen. He put out his arm to prevent her.

"Were you asleep?"

"No." She didn't even convince herself with that answer.

Simon stepped back and walked to the front door. But instead of leaving, he turned the lock and flipped over the sign to Closed.

"What are you doing? I don't close for another hour."

"Tonight, you're closing early."

"Last time I checked, you weren't the boss around here."

"And last time I checked, I wasn't falling asleep on the job."

"I dozed off, okay? What's the big deal?"

He stalked toward her, stopping just a step away. "It's a big deal because someone could walk in here and rob you blind or worse."

"Don't be so dramatic. This is Blue Falls."

He reached out and gripped her shoulders. "Crime happens everywhere, Keri."

When she looked up at him, she was shocked to see genuine concern in his eyes. She didn't want him to care, because it was easier to stay mad at him. But something about his touch and strength finally robbed her of her last bit of resolve.

"I'm just so tired," she said. "I can't remember the last time I got a good night of sleep."

"Well, you will tonight."

She shook her head slowly. "Hannah will be awake in the middle of the night. I shouldn't let her nap so much during the day, but it makes working so much easier."

Simon lifted her chin, forcing her to look at him. "You can't keep doing this. Tonight, you sleep. I'll watch after Hannah."

She stared at him, not understanding.

"I'll sleep on the couch, keep Hannah in the room with me. That way, you can sleep through the night."

"Simon, this isn't your responsibility."

"And you don't have to do everything alone. For once, stop being so damned stubborn."

She bit her lip to keep from crying at the mere idea of a full night of sleep.

Though part of her brain was screaming at her that she was making a huge mistake, she let Simon help her finish closing and then drive her and Hannah home. When they walked in the front door, all she wanted to do was make a beeline for her bed.

"Are you hungry?" she asked instead.

"I'm sure I can scrounge up something."

"More like you'll set my house on fire."

"You forget I'm a bachelor. I'd starve if I couldn't make something."

She laughed. "Somehow I doubt you have to make many meals for yourself."

He set Hannah down to crawl on the floor, then took off his hat and ran his fingers through his hair. "I'm not sure what you mean, Miss Mehler."

She crossed her arms and leaned against the side of the couch. "Just that between your mom, two sisters-in-law and your many, many girlfriends, I'm guessing you're pretty well covered."

"My many, many girlfriends?"

"Yes, evidently the combination of cowboy and man in uniform is attractive to the female population of Blue Falls. Is there any woman of legal age and who isn't old enough to be your grandmother that you haven't dated?"

"You."

With that one word, the air in the room changed. Suddenly, having this man spend the night in her home seemed like the worst of ideas. She doubted even walls and doors would be enough to keep out the tension vibrating between them.

Keri pushed away from the couch. "Well, if you're sure you're okay, I think I will turn in."

After changing Hannah's diaper and putting her in her little pink pj's, Keri placed her in her bouncy seat and left Simon to his babysitting.

Despite her extreme fatigue, however, she found it hard to fall asleep knowing Simon was just down the hallway.

Though she couldn't understand what he said, she could hear the soft rumble of his voice as he talked to Hannah. Here, in the privacy of her room, she was tempted to admit what she'd been feeling all day. That she was intensely attracted to Simon, could imagine him pulling her into his arms and kissing her senseless.

But what in the world could she do about it? He was still the reason her brother was out there somewhere with a police record and no idea his oldest sister was dead.

No matter how much she told herself she should hate him, her body and imagination kept betraying her. She grabbed the extra pillow and hugged it close as she curled onto her side, letting herself imagine what it might be like to hold an actual warm body next to her instead of a cool, lifeless pillow.

A warm body that looked remarkably like Simon Teague's.

Chapter Six

Keri woke the next morning to the smell of bacon. For a moment, she flashed back to mornings when her mother had prepared breakfast for the family. A pang of sorrow hit her, but it was one with which she'd become accustomed. The much fresher, rawer pain of Sammi's death caused her to close her eyes and try to will it to not be true.

Despite thoughts of her family, she realized that she felt much better this morning. Once she'd fallen asleep, she'd been out for the count. When was the last time she'd ever slept the entire night through without even waking to go to the bathroom? She stretched and enjoyed the feeling of being rested for a couple more minutes before consulting the clock and realizing she had to get going. Life started early when you ran a bakery.

After showering and getting dressed, she made her way toward the kitchen. As she drew close, she stopped and listened.

"So, Hannah, what do you think I should get my new niece when she's born?"

Hannah jabbered something unintelligible.

"Now, you're going to have to be more specific than that. You being a girl and all, you've got to help a guy out."

Keri grinned before rounding the corner into the kitchen.

"I think your niece will be needing a good supply of diapers and baby wipes," she said.

"Well, that's no fun," Simon said as he glanced up from the stove. Hannah smacked her little hands repeatedly against the tray of her high chair. "See, Hannah agrees. I'm thinking I can't go wrong with my plan for favorite uncle status if I start off with toys."

Keri shook her head as she crossed the room to the coffeepot. "That child is going to be spoiled rotten."

"Yep."

She tried to nab a piece of bacon, but he shooed her away.

"Hey, I believe that's my food you're cooking."

"And since I'm the cook this morning, my rules."

She raised her eyebrows at him but played along, taking her cup of coffee and heading to the table.

"Hannah, why did we ever let this crazy man in the house?"

Hannah responded with a slobbery grin.

Keri looked up in time to see Simon giving her a look she couldn't quite peg. "What?"

"Nothing." But he smiled as he turned back toward the stove to flip a pancake.

When he slid a plate of pancakes and bacon in front of her, her stomach responded by growling.

"Just in time, by the sound of it," he said.

She almost stuck her tongue out at him, but that felt too much like old times, as though everything was just hunky-dory with them again. But despite their unspoken truce, she couldn't just erase how she felt about what he'd done, what he'd cost her and her family.

So she didn't say anything but dug into her breakfast.

After a bite of pancakes covered in warm syrup and a piece of crisp bacon, she moaned in appreciation before she could stop herself.

"Told you I could cook," he said as he slid into the chair opposite her with his own plate. He looked so satisfied with himself that she very nearly threw half a slice of bacon at him. He gave her a mischievous grin that did funny things to her insides.

"It's edible."

Instead of putting more of a barrier between them, her words just made him smile wider.

The sound of the cell phone strapped to his belt drew his attention, allowing her to breathe a little easier.

"Where?" he asked into the phone, suddenly all business.

He stood and walked into the living room Rebelling against her common sense, her gaze drifted to his backside and down his long legs. He'd grown up on a horse, so she had no doubt those legs had a strong grip. She squirmed in her seat at the sudden desire to find out.

So many more important things should be occupying her mind, and yet way too many images of Simon fought for space there. The little devil on her shoulder whispered, "What can it hurt to fantasize a little?" The smarter, more cautious angel on the other shoulder said, "Not smart to yearn for things that can never be."

She tore off a bite of one of her pancakes and handed it to Hannah. "Don't tell him I said so, but these are darn good pancakes."

She wondered if he'd learned to make them from his mother. Or maybe Grace or Brooke, his sisters-in-law. Childish and stupid as it might be, she hoped it wasn't from one of the women whose bed he'd warmed—like she'd fantasized about him warming hers the night before.

When he walked back into the kitchen, she shoved hot, sweaty images of him away.

"I'm sorry, but I'm going to have to go."

"Everything okay?"

"Duty calls again."

She nodded and carried the dishes to the sink. "Let me grab Hannah's diaper bag and I'll be ready."

"Sorry to rush you."

"No, it's okay. Goodness knows I have plenty to do at work myself."

When Simon pulled up in front of the bakery a few minutes later, she slid out and unhooked Hannah's car seat. She started to shut the door but paused. "Simon?"

"Yeah?"

"Thank you for last night. I didn't realize how close I was to collapsing."

He nodded. "You're welcome."

"And for cooking breakfast."

"That's got to be good for a week of free doughnuts and coffee, don't you think?"

She smiled and shook her head. "Don't push it."

He was laughing as she closed the door and watched him drive on down the street toward the sheriff's department. When she turned toward the bakery, she noticed the interior lights were on. Then she saw Sunshine inside.

Her cheerful mood evaporated. She'd banked on getting to work early enough that no one would notice who'd been her chauffeur and wonder about it. Well, no help for it now.

She acted as if nothing was out of the ordinary as she walked in the front door. "I thought you were sick," she said, closing the door behind her.

"Felt some better this morning and knew you needed

the help. Imagine my surprise when I heard from Justine that you'd had plenty of help yesterday."

"Nothing like you. I'm glad you're back."

"Uh-huh," Sunshine said, her response rife with skepticism. She motioned out the front window. "So, care to explain that?"

Keri headed for the office to place Hannah in the playpen. "Nothing to explain. For some reason, he's just been helping me out."

"Why was he dropping you off this morning? I got here and saw your car, but no you."

"He babysat for me last night so I could get some sleep."

"At your house?"

"Yes, at my house. And for your information, he slept on the couch. And I finally got a decent night's sleep."

"Well, you're either a better woman than me or blind because there's no way I could sleep if that man was in my house. Other things maybe, but no sleeping."

Keri's mouth dropped open.

"Don't look so surprised. I'm a happily married woman and way too old for him, but that doesn't mean I can't see that Simon Teague is sex on two very long legs."

Heat rushed up Keri's throat to her face.

"And I see from your reaction that you've had the same thought."

Keri pushed past Sunshine into the kitchen.

"Haven't you?" her friend persisted.

Keri threw up her hands. "Yes, okay, but it's not right."

"Because of your tiff with him?"

"It was more than a tiff."

"Whatever it is, maybe it's time you let it go. Kids do stupid things. And then they grow up."

With a shake of her head, Keri started pulling out

ingredients for cherry cream cheese pastries. "Doesn't matter. I can't go down that road now."

"Because you're too busy or because you think it's too soon?"

"Both."

Sunshine went back to work on the tray of cinnamon rolls she'd been in the midst of making when Keri had arrived. "Here's the thing—you're always going to be busy. You've got a business to run and a child to raise. Don't fool yourself that things will slow down at some point." She paused to slip the tray into the top oven, then turned to face Keri. "As for the other, I think maybe now is exactly when you need someone."

"I can't think about a man now. My sister just died."

"I know, and it's awful. But can you stand there and tell me that Sammi would have wanted you to put your life on hold?"

"I don't know."

"I think she would have wanted you to find someone and be as happy as she was with Ben."

Keri closed her eyes against an image of Sammi's wedding day, of how happy she'd been as she'd stared at her new husband. She'd been absolutely aglow with love. Keri remembered wondering what that kind of love would feel like. But as the years passed she'd begun to believe the Mehler girls had used up their allotment of luck in the romance department when Sammi had found Ben.

Thankfully, Sunshine walked away and left Keri to work. And think way too much about what her friend had just said, and how she'd liked walking into the kitchen that morning and seeing Simon there.

Damn, why couldn't she be attracted to someone else? As she so often did when she didn't want to deal with life outside her little baking bubble, she threw herself into work.

About midmorning, she looked up to see Merline Teague, Simon's mother, walking in the front door with a stack of flyers.

"Good morning, girls," Merline said with a little wave.

She and Sunshine responded with their own greetings.

"What can I get for you?" Keri asked as she stepped to the counter.

"I'll take a large coffee and a slice of the iced coffee cake. And can I leave some flyers here for Christmas in Blue Falls?"

"Sure." Keri reached into the display case and pulled out the coffee cake.

"Will you be taking part this year?"

Keri sensed some hesitance in Merline's question, and it was obvious why. She'd received the same careful consideration from everyone, including the tellers at the bank and the checkers at the H-E-B.

"Yeah, that's always a great event. Put us down for having free Christmas cookies, coffee and hot cider."

"Wonderful." Merline pulled a notebook out of her purse.

Christmas in Blue Falls was the local chamber of commerce's effort to get locals and tourists alike to spend the entire day in town shopping for Christmas presents, visiting the live nativity at St. Pius Church, eating in the town's restaurants and watching the annual Christmas parade and tree-lighting ceremony. She'd been enjoying the festivities each year for as long as she could remember. But despite her willingness to take part, she couldn't drum up any excitement this time around. Sammi and Ben had always come down from Dallas that weekend, and she was afraid the festivities were going to yawn with emptiness from now on. Honestly, she just wanted the holidays to be over.

Merline met her at the cash register, but after the exchange of goods for cash was completed the other woman lingered.

"Can I get you anything else?" Keri asked.

"If you don't have plans for Thanksgiving, I'd like to invite you to spend the day with us."

Surprise registered just before the realization that she'd been so busy and preoccupied lately that she hadn't realized Thanksgiving was only a few days away.

"That's kind of you, but—"

"No buts," Merline said with a warm smile. "We're going to have more food than we can possibly eat, and you need a day when you don't have to cook or bake a single thing."

Keri struggled with conflicted feelings. She was used to spending Thanksgiving surrounded by family, however small, so staying home alone with Hannah held little appeal. But would being in the midst of such a big, loving family only make her sorrow that much deeper?

She found herself agreeing to the invitation. "But I can't come empty-handed."

"You won't be. You'll have little Hannah, and we do love to dote on babies. It'll give us a little practice before Nathan and Grace's baby arrives."

"When is she due?"

"Around Christmas."

The image of the entire Teague family around a brightly lit Christmas tree, oohing and ahhing over a brand-new baby, caused a lump to form in Keri's throat. The image was so perfect it hurt to think she would never have that for herself. That Sammi and Ben had been cheated out of witnessing their baby's first Christmas.

"We'll be eating around noon, but feel free to come out early."

Keri nodded just as the squawl of an ambulance siren drew their attention outside. The ambulance zipped by in a flash of red and white.

"Well, that doesn't look good," Sunshine said as she came to the front and slid a new batch of snickerdoodles into the display case.

Keri's stomach clenched as she imagined a similar ambulance racing toward the scene of Sammi and Ben's wreck only to find the trip had been in vain. *Killed at the scene.* The words echoed in her mind, causing her to feel sick and weak. She hated feeling this way, as though she'd been scraped raw inside. Then she hated herself for the momentary wish that the worst of the grieving could be over, that she could get through a day without thinking of her sister every five seconds.

After Merline left, Keri and Sunshine fell into a familiar rhythm and Keri took a measure of comfort from it. When the UPS truck pulled up outside for the daily pickup, she scooped up a pile of boxes to help Erik carry them out. As soon as she stepped out onto the sidewalk, a sheriff's department car raced by with the siren blaring.

"What's going on?" she wondered aloud.

"Looked like something about five miles out of town," Erik said as he rounded the back of the truck and opened the rear doors. "I passed several police cars and an ambulance, and they were diverting traffic through a detour."

A knot of dread settled in her stomach like a stone on the bottom of a pond. She couldn't shake the feeling as she busied herself with work. Around lunchtime, Jo Baker strolled in the front door. Normally, she could have lived without Jo's business just fine. But if anyone knew what was going on this morning, it'd be Jo.

"Hello, Jo. What can I get you?"

"Just a cup of coffee." She appeared distracted by a text message on her phone. When she looked up, she had that look of someone about to spill juicy gossip. "Seems there was a big drug bust this morning."

Keri swallowed her normal distaste for gossip. "So, that's what all the ruckus has been about?" She thought about the ambulance. "Anyone hurt?"

"Yeah, a friend of mine heard on her police scanner that a cop was shot."

Keri's thoughts immediately went to Simon, and she had to grip the edge of the countertop to steady herself.

"Any idea who?" That had to be where Simon had gone earlier.

Jo shook her head and nabbed her coffee. Her work of spreading news done, she left.

Keri stood staring out the window at all the residents of Blue Falls going about their daily business as if nothing out of the ordinary had happened. As if someone who was sworn to protect them hadn't taken a bullet.

She jumped when Sunshine placed her hand against her back.

"You don't know it's him. I'm sure there were at least a dozen cops on a raid like that."

Keri blinked against tears she hadn't expected, nodded and went to her office to check on Hannah. Though she'd been deliberately keeping her distance, she scooped up her niece and held her close, as if the universe might try to snatch her away when Keri wasn't looking. Fate had an ugly habit of doing that.

Despite the work that still waited for her, she sat in her office and held Hannah for the longest time. She fought the urge to call the hospital to find out who'd been shot—how would she explain her need to know? Of course, they wouldn't tell her, anyway. She considered calling Simon but didn't know his cell number. As the minutes ticked by, she realized that she wasn't sure she wanted to find out who'd been shot. As it stood now, the possibility that Simon was okay still existed. If she found out he'd been shot, that possibility would be gone.

Even considering that thought, she turned on the radio. The news at the top of the hour revealed that UT was planning a distinguished alumni reunion, more bad weather was hitting the Plains and cases of brutal coyotes—human smugglers—across the border were increasing as the living conditions and danger level in Mexico worsened.

But there was nothing about the drug bust or shooting. When the news ended, Keri switched off the radio.

"That's awful how those smugglers take advantage of people's desperation," Sunshine said as she shook her head. She was likely trying to get Keri's mind off the shooting, but that didn't make her words any less true.

Keri nodded in agreement but couldn't focus on the plight of others when all her worry was reserved for Simon.

Somehow she went through the motions that got her through the rest of the day. At about six o'clock, she eyed Sunshine, who was affixing labels to more shipping boxes.

"Doesn't Brett have a game tonight?"

"Yeah."

"You're going to miss the tip-off. I can finish up here."

Sunshine waved her hand. "He's got lots of other games."

Keri turned more fully toward her friend and placed her hand on her hip, making a show of strength she didn't feel. "You have never missed one of Brett's games. Now get out of here."

"I don't want to leave you by yourself."

"I think I can manage a slow hour at the end of the day."

Sunshine was on the verge of saying something else before she changed her mind. "Fine, but you call if you need anything."

"Go, cheer, give the refs a hard time."

Sunshine smiled. "I'm not that bad."

"I hear refs tremble in their squeaky black shoes when they see you in the stands."

Sunshine rolled her eyes, grabbed her purse from under the counter and headed out the door.

Keri kept up the facade of being okay until Sunshine was out of sight. The not knowing if Simon was safe had worn her down to the point where the lovely rest she'd gotten the night before was a distant memory. As she cleaned surfaces that had already been wiped down, she tried to figure out why it mattered so much. Of course, despite her years of being angry at him she didn't want him to be shot.

But it was more than that, wasn't it? Somehow he was carving out a spot for himself in her life, and she didn't mind.

A couple of minutes after Sunshine left, the front door opened. When she looked up, there stood Simon in his uniform, safe and whole. She released the mass of concern that had been her companion all day. Though she ached to run to him and make sure he was okay, she returned her attention to the table and flicked imaginary lint off the top of the large mixer.

"I just ran into Sunshine," he said as he closed the distance between them. "She said you wanted to talk to me."

"Oh," she said, scrambling for something to say. "No, I…"

As he drew closer, her sense of self-preservation screamed at her to move away. But her feet refused to listen.

"Keri, what's wrong?"

"I'm glad you're okay," she said quietly without looking up.

He edged closer, so close she could lean against him with little effort. He placed his hand on her shoulder and turned her to face him. "What are you talking about?"

Though she feared looking into his eyes with him so close, she lifted her gaze to his. "I heard an officer got shot, and…"

"You thought it might be me."

She lowered her eyes and nodded.

"And that would bother you?" he asked, a bit of laughter in his voice, likely at the idea that she would care at all about what happened to him.

"Yes."

Something indefinable changed in his stance, and he slid his hand along her jaw, forcing her to meet his eyes again.

"I'm fine. Some guy running a meth lab took exception to us paying a visit and he got off a shot, hit one of the state guys in the leg. But he's okay. We all are."

Simon let his hand drift up to smooth the hair at her temple.

"I'm sorry you worried," he said.

Her mouth opened but she had no idea what to say, what to do. The gentleness of his touch and the sincerity in his words made her heart beat a little faster than normal. She knew it would be the biggest bad move of her life, but she wanted nothing more than to kiss him in that moment. When his gaze met hers again, she saw a similar thought reflected there. It sent a shock wave of common sense through her and she stepped away from Simon, breaking all contact so she would have a hope of thinking straight.

"Why do you do that?" he asked.

"Wha—?"

"Deliberately keep your distance."

"I don't know what you mean."

He closed the space she'd placed between them. "I think you do."

"Listen, I'm just glad you didn't get yourself shot, okay?"

"And it's not just me you do it with," he continued. "You've pulled away from Hannah, too, whether you realize it or not."

"I can't just be the fun aunt anymore. I'm responsible for her welfare."

"That's not it."

Why was he pressing this issue? It wasn't any of his business. Offering a little help around the bakery didn't give him the right to tell her how to live her life or how to raise Hannah.

She straightened her spine and met his gaze dead-on. "Just because you're a cop, don't think you know everything about everyone. You're not always right."

He stared at her as the weight of her words hung in the air. Neither of them had to say anything to know they'd just been propelled back to when she'd told him she hated him for what he'd done to Carter.

"You're not, either."

Chapter Seven

"I was with him that day." He pressed on despite the "I knew it" look in her eyes. "But I wasn't the one to spray paint the house. I tried to get him to stop, but he wouldn't listen."

"That doesn't make sense. You were the one Mrs. Abbott was upset with that day."

"And Carter was mad at her on my behalf."

"Why would he take that kind of risk?"

Here it was, the truth he'd kept to himself all these years. "Because he thought it was funny. Because he thought he could get away with it the way he had everything else."

"What are you talking about? What 'everything else'?"

Simon rubbed his hand over his face, wishing this conversation were over.

"Simon?"

"You remember when the water tower got spray painted with that rather rude picture?"

She thought for a moment then nodded.

"That was Carter. And so was the time Mayor Aldrich's car got egged while he was parked at Daisy Stone's house." Daisy was not Mrs. Aldrich.

"You're telling me my brother's a criminal?"

"Yes. At least he did some things that were misdemeanors, criminal mischief. And you know he's had arrests since he left."

"Why didn't you stop him?"

"I tried, but he wouldn't listen. He said I was just afraid my parents would find out. And he was right about that." He paused and wished he could go back in time so he could try harder to set Carter straight. "I saw him spray paint that house, but when I heard sirens I ran. I'm not proud of it, but it's what happened."

"You didn't tell the police you were there."

"No, I didn't."

"But you didn't tell them it was Carter, either." He saw when the reality of her misperception clicked into place. "Why not?"

"One, it would have put me at the crime scene, too. And…well, I just couldn't rat him out, especially since he didn't mention I was there. But I couldn't lie and say he was somewhere he wasn't, either."

Keri ran her hand through her hair as she paced a few steps to her right before stopping and meeting his eyes again. "Why didn't you tell me?"

"I tried, but you wouldn't listen. You'd already made up your mind about me. And to tell you the truth, it made me mad, too."

"You should have kept trying."

"What was I supposed to do, push you up against a wall and hold you there until you believed me?"

She gestured outward with her hands as though she was at a loss for the right answer. "I don't know, but if I'd known the truth maybe I could have talked some sense into him before he got himself into more trouble."

"He wouldn't have listened."

"How do you know that?"

"Because I'd tried until I was blue in the face to get

him to stop doing stupid stuff. But every time he got away with it, it gave him a high and he wanted to do something even bigger."

"You make him sound awful."

"No, I'm just telling you the truth. That's what you wanted."

She looked so haunted in that moment that he ached to pull her into his arms, but he suspected that gesture wouldn't be welcome.

"I believe Carter's a good guy at heart," he said. "I mean, he was my best friend. He just has some issues." Serious ones.

"Ones my parents didn't know how to deal with." Her voice sounded so sad it broke his heart. "I overheard them arguing one night. And my parents never argued. Mom wanted to give Carter another chance, but Dad was done. Carter had just been arrested for drinking out at Biggins Rock," she said, referencing a popular hiking area in the western edge of the county. "Dad told Carter he had to shape up or leave. I don't think he actually thought Carter would go."

He pretty much knew the rest of the story. Carter moved from place to place and job to job and popped into town for occasional visits, usually when he was low on funds.

"As hard as it is to do, sometimes you have to let people make their own mistakes and just hope they stumble upon the right path at some point," he said.

Though he'd pretty much given up on that for Carter, he wasn't about to tell Keri that. She'd lost too much. She deserved to hang on to her hope for her brother, even if it proved fruitless in the end.

Quiet settled around them as Keri stared down at the floor. As the moments stretched, he listened to the sounds of the heating unit switching on, the ticking of the clock on the wall and the thrumming of his own pulse.

"You let me stay angry at you all these years," she finally said.

"After a while, it just got to be the norm. And I didn't see it changing."

"Sammi always said I was too hard on you. Even Carter told me to let it go. But I couldn't."

"I understand. You love your brother."

She looked up at him then. "I do, but…I think maybe I knew I was being unreasonable somewhere deep down. I was the only one holding the grudge." She looked away and seemingly stared at nothing for the longest time. "I think it hurt me more not just because of Carter, but because of you."

He watched her, trying to understand what she was saying.

"Because you thought I'd ruined our friendship," he said.

"It was more than that." She swallowed visibly. "I liked you, as more than a friend."

For a guy who had to be observant in his job, that one had flown right by him. "I didn't know."

"Of course you didn't. I didn't let it show. Sammi was the only one who figured it out, and I swore her to secrecy."

She lowered her gaze again and picked at her fingernails. "I'm sorry I was so awful to you."

"There's no need to apologize. It's not like I'm blameless in this. If I could go back in time, I'd find a way to stop him, get through to him before he ruined his life."

"Unfortunately, we can't go back in time."

He knew Carter's string of run-ins with the law wasn't the only thing Keri was thinking she'd like to change.

Hoping he wasn't pushing her a step too far, he asked, "Still no word from him?"

She shook her head. No matter what had happened in the past, her inability to reach her brother to tell him about Sammi ate at her. Hell, it ate at him, too. He'd had more resources at his disposal, and he still couldn't find the guy. It was as if he'd just vanished.

"I've looked, too."

"You have?"

He had to admit it hurt that she sounded so surprised. "Yeah. Unfortunately, no luck yet. But I'll keep trying."

"Thank you."

Though they'd cleared the air and Keri seemed to accept the truth, the ensuing quiet grew awkward. Maybe the truth wasn't enough to make everything right between them. His anger flared, but Keri wasn't the target. No, it was the brother who'd done nothing for years but think of himself.

Once again, Carter Mehler was coming between them, even when he was nowhere to be found.

"I HAVE TO WORK TOMORROW," Simon said as he walked toward the filing cabinet in his office to put away some paperwork.

"Not until tomorrow night, you don't," his mom said. "I already checked the schedule with Jack."

"Remind me to fire him."

"What's wrong? I thought you and Keri were getting along again. I heard you were even helping her out at the bakery."

"Nothing's wrong." Unless you counted how difficult it was to give Keri the space she needed while also thinking that since he'd seen her last she might have decided to never speak to him again.

"Did you tell her the truth?"

"Yes. And it didn't magically make everything okay."

"I never said it would. Just give her time to digest everything. She'll come around."

"I love you, but this time I think you might be wrong."

She pulled her purse onto her shoulder and gave him one of her mother-knows-all looks. "We'll see."

When she left, he dropped into his chair and ran his hand over his face. Unless all hell broke loose the next day, there was no getting out of having to face Keri at his family's Thanksgiving meal. With Nathan and Ryan married off, his mom had set her sights on finding the perfect woman for him. If she was thinking that woman was Keri Mehler, she'd lost her marbles somewhere along the way.

But he might be doing the avoidance dance for no reason. Keri could cancel and not even be there. Why was he working himself into knots over a woman who would never be more than a friend at best?

But if Keri was so wrong for him, why did he miss her? Why, after several years of practice at avoiding her, was it suddenly difficult to not stop in at the bakery each morning for coffee, a pastry and a chance to see her?

He was done. If trying to bury the hatchet and start over as friends didn't appeal to her, fine. He'd get through tomorrow the way he had living in the same small town as her all these years—pure and simple avoidance. There would be plenty of other people there to keep her occupied.

And if part of him still wanted to get near her, he'd smack it down for the fool it was. She'd made her feelings quite clear.

Time to get back in the dating game, to find someone to make him feel normal again.

Yeah, because that had worked out so well the other

night when he'd gone to the music hall with Justine. He'd told Keri that Justine canceled. In truth, they'd called it an early night because Justine was a smart woman and could tell he was only half there. His really stupid half had been with Keri, wanting to help and protect the woman who'd never made any secret of how little she cared about him.

Then why had she been so concerned the other day when she'd thought he might be shot? There was no reason for her to feign worry for him, and what he'd seen in her eyes had been the real thing.

He let his head drop back against his chair and closed his eyes, rubbing them with his thumb and forefinger. Some women were just way too hard to figure out.

When the phone rang, Nathan's number came up on the caller ID.

"Cops R Us," he answered.

His brother snorted. "We still playing cards tonight?"

"Yeah." Maybe more than a date, he actually needed a guy night—some poker, cold beer and humor not appreciated by the females in their lives.

But as he, his brothers and Pete, one of his deputies, sat around his scuffed kitchen table that night, he fought the urge to curse. And it wasn't because he was on the worst poker streak ever.

"What's eating you?" Nathan asked. "You're playing like you've never seen a deck of cards before."

"Anything to do with who Mom invited to Thanksgiving dinner?" Ryan asked.

Simon didn't spare either of his brothers a glance. "Mom can invite whoever she wants. It's her house."

"So, it doesn't bother you that Keri will be there?" Ryan asked.

"Why should it?"

"Heard you've been spending a lot of time with her lately."

This is what he got for teasing and pushing Ryan to make a move with Brooke. Payback time had evidently arrived.

"What, you and Jo Baker suddenly best buds?"

"No, but word gets around."

Simon rearranged his dud of a hand. It was as if his mood was rubbing off on his cards. "In case you haven't noticed, she's had a bad month. I've just lent a hand a couple of times."

"All night, at her house?"

Blasted small town where everyone knew everyone's business. He tossed his cards down in disgust.

He eyed both of his brothers with an accusing glare. "Getting married has obviously turned your brains to mush." Then he made the mistake of looking at Pete, who was still single.

Pete shrugged. "Dude, you've got the hots for her. Anyone can see it."

Simon swung his forefinger between Ryan and Nathan. "These two I'm stuck with." Then he pointed at Pete. "You, I can fire your ass."

Pete snorted, which set all three guys to laughing.

Simon called them all a couple of unflattering names before tossing his empty beer bottle toward the trash can. He missed and the bottle rolled across the kitchen floor before coming to rest against the bottom of the refrigerator.

"Looks like your aim could use some work."

Simon was smart enough to figure out Nathan wasn't only talking about his trash can basketball skills, or lack thereof.

Did he, as Pete said, have the hots for Keri? And if so, what the devil was he supposed to do about it?

As KERI DROVE INTO THE Vista Hills Ranch, she wondered if she'd lost her mind. Yes, she'd decided to attempt to move forward, but she still wasn't sure how she felt about Simon. And spending the day in the same house as him didn't seem like the smartest thing when her feelings were still so jumbled. The moment he'd walked out of the bakery the other night, she'd wanted to call him back, to be able to erase all the bad things that had happened between them. She'd wanted desperately for them to have never had a reason, real or perceived, to end their friendship.

When the house came into view, she felt like an interloper. Today was a day for family gatherings, and she was going to stick out like the proverbial sore thumb. She'd changed her mind about coming today about a dozen times since she'd gotten up at the crack of dawn, unable to sleep.

She shook her head as she parked in front of the ranch office. She'd gotten through worse things than this. Managing an uncomfortable holiday gathering was the least of her worries.

When she got Hannah's carrier unhooked from its base in the backseat, she slung the diaper bag over her shoulder, then picked up the carrier with one hand and the red velvet cake she'd made with the other. By the time she reached the front door, her arms were shaking and she didn't have any hands left to knock. Luckily, Brooke saw her and opened the door.

"You've got your hands full," the lovely brunette said. "Let me take that." She reached for the cake holder.

"Oh, let me see that baby," Merline said as she walked

across the great room from the kitchen. "Hey there, little one. Aren't you just the prettiest thing?"

"I'm really worried she's not going to get this doting grandmother thing down," Nathan said, his voice rich with sarcasm.

"You better hope I do."

Keri smiled at the easy laughter. She still felt out of place, but the reality wasn't as bad as the anticipation. She scanned the room and saw everyone but Simon. Maybe he was working. She supposed crime never took a holiday.

"Here, let's get you out of that thing," Merline said as she unhooked Hannah's restraints and pulled her into her arms. "I do love the smell of a baby."

"Well, she doesn't smell good all the time," Keri said. The occasional diaper changing had been one thing. Now that all the diaper changings were up to her, she marveled at how many times a baby managed to go to the bathroom.

Merline smiled at her. "The good news is they eventually learn to take care of that kind of thing all on their own."

Keri looked ahead to a future full of potty training, helping with homework, parent-teacher conferences, the birds-and-bees discussion and giving too-interested boys the evil eye. If she let it, the weight of all that responsibility would cause her to collapse.

"Hank, honey, take Keri's coat," Merline said.

Merline's husband did just that, then poked at Hannah's little nose in a gesture that was so similar to his oldest son's that Keri had to look away. As the members of the Teague family took turns holding and playing with Hannah, Keri wandered into the kitchen.

"Can I help with anything?"

"No, we have everything covered," Grace said from her perch on a high stool next to the island.

"How are you feeling?" Keri asked Nathan's wife.

"Like I swallowed a beach ball with legs."

Keri smiled, though the image was accompanied with a memory of Sammi saying something very similar when she'd been pregnant with Hannah.

After handing Hannah off to Nathan, Merline walked up to the kitchen island and pecked on the top of Keri's cake carrier with a fingernail. "I thought I said you didn't have to bring anything."

"Sorry, that's just not in my makeup. My mama taught me to never show up at a gathering empty-handed."

"Very well." Merline lifted the lid. "What have we got in here?"

"Red velvet cake with cream cheese frosting."

"Oh, we'll have to hide this from Simon or he'll have half of it eaten before we get the turkey out of the oven. It's his favorite."

Of course it was. Had that little tidbit been stored somewhere in the back of her brain and she'd tapped into it without knowing? She just hoped that wasn't what he ended up thinking whenever he showed up. Because it sounded like he was expected at this get-together. She guessed he had the power to charge his underlings with working on holidays so he was free.

Behind her, she heard Hannah beginning to fuss. But before she could turn around, a familiar voice said, "Oh, now, none of that. Come to me, little princess."

"Well, would you look at that," Brooke said as she looked past Keri to where Simon was no doubt showering Hannah with all kinds of attention.

Grace laughed. "His ability to charm the female population knows no bounds."

Keri ignored their comments and Simon's presence in the house. She couldn't admit that for a moment in time, she, too, had been susceptible to Simon's flirtatious, sexy magnetism. Still might be. The man ought to come with a warning label.

Though the Teague women told her that she was a guest and therefore exempt from kitchen duty, Keri threw herself into helping nonetheless. Anything to keep her from having to acknowledge Simon or make eye contact with him. As she carried a bowl of green beans into the dining room, she noticed a high chair sitting at one corner of the table.

Grace walked in after her with a platter of ham. "That was Evan's when he was a baby," she said.

"I didn't even think about bringing Hannah's."

Grace squeezed her hand. "Don't worry. You'll eventually get used to everything."

Keri wasn't so sure about that. She hadn't had the benefit of the nine months moms had to prepare for a baby. She had all the paraphernalia but not the mental readiness. During the entirety of Hannah's life, Keri had thought of herself as the cool aunt who could spoil her niece with presents then give her back to her mother. Now, she'd been thrust into the unwilling role of mother without any right to call herself that.

Once all of the food was on the long dining room table Merline ushered everyone to their seats. Keri stopped moving when she noticed she'd been placed next to Simon. But there was no way out of it without making a scene and drawing attention to the fact that she had a problem with the seating arrangement. And she wasn't going to mess up Thanksgiving for the Teagues, not when they'd all been kind to her and Hannah. Including Simon, him most of all.

Part of her acknowledged that his kindnesses toward her niece had softened her perception of him, even before he'd made his confession and she'd realized she'd been wrong about so much. The part of her that still resisted whispered that he wasn't totally without fault. After all, he'd looked out for himself at her brother's expense.

But maybe he was just tired of covering for him.

Keri slid into her seat, still without making eye contact. She could make it through this. It was just a meal, a bit of socializing, and then she could escape back to the relative safety of her home.

Her heart thumped a bit harder when she looked to the opposite side of the table and noticed Nathan, Grace and Evan clasping hands. A quick glance around the table revealed everyone else was offering up their hands, too, for the prayer of thanks. Then she noticed Simon's hand sitting, palm-up, between his plate and hers. Reluctantly, she raised her own hand and placed it in his.

Heat shot up her arm as his fingers closed around hers. If they were alone, she'd be tempted to close her eyes and savor the feeling of masculine strength and work-roughened texture. Instead, she reached out her other hand and took Hannah's, then lowered her head as Hank offered up the blessing.

When the prayer was over, she didn't snatch her hand from Simon's but she also didn't linger. Doing either would reveal too much about how he made her feel against her will.

Though the food was good, Keri had lost most of her appetite. There was hardly room within her for anything other than the tension that was flowing back and forth between her and Simon.

"Have you thought about fixing up a room for Hannah yet?" Grace asked from the other side of the table.

"Pardon?"

Grace nodded at Hannah. "I've seen a lot of rooms that

can start out as nurseries and be easily converted to rooms
for older kids. If you're interested, I can come over sometime and show you some ideas."

Honestly, she'd given it no thought at all. For now,
Hannah was sleeping in her crib in Keri's room. Though
Hannah had had her own room at Sammi's house, Keri
couldn't sleep in a separate room, afraid she wouldn't hear
Hannah if she cried. She was irrationally terrified that if
the baby was in a different room, she might disappear in
the night without Keri knowing.

"Um, maybe after the holidays."

"I hear things have really been busy at the bakery,"
Merline said from farther down the table. "Erik Thompson swears he's going to have to start bringing a bigger
UPS truck to town to pick up all the boxes you're shipping out of there."

"This is a really crazy time of year," Keri replied. Not
to mention she'd gotten a late start due to fate interven-
ing. And the fact that her head hadn't been fully engaged
in her work since before Simon had shown up outside the
bakery that snowy night with the news that had shattered
her world.

"I was glad to hear Simon helped you out some," Merline said.

Keri felt Simon stop moving next to her at the same
time a jolt of awkwardness shot through her. "Yes, that
was very helpful." Good grief, she felt like a very hot
spotlight was being directed right at her.

"Can Hannah have some sweet potatoes?" Brooke
asked.

Keri turned her attention to the other woman seated on
the opposite side of Hannah and saw the bowl of mashed
sweet potatoes in front of her. "Sure. But I don't know if
she likes them." Admitting that embarrassed her and made

her feel as if she wasn't fit to raise Hannah. Doubt crept through her until it was difficult to sit still.

Brooke attempted to feed Hannah a spoonful of sweet potatoes, but as soon as she tasted them Hannah screwed up her face and stuck out her tongue.

"Well, I guess that answers that question," Nathan said, and everyone laughed.

Even Keri managed a slight smile. She envied the easy laughter and wondered if she would ever truly laugh again.

When it looked like everyone was finished eating, Keri stood to help clear the table. This time, no one tried to stop her from helping for which she was grateful. When the table was clear, Merline grabbed dessert plates while Grace got the forks and a pumpkin pie. Brooke took hold of a carrot cake and serving utensils.

"Bring your cake," she said to Keri.

"That's okay. Looks like you all have enough dessert already."

"Nonsense," Merline said from the dining room and waved her in. "Simon, Keri made a red velvet cake."

Before she could stop herself, Keri met Simon's gaze. It was the first time she'd allowed herself to look at him all day, and fate laughed at her by having him take her breath away. He wore a blue shirt that she knew had to bring out the color of his eyes. Before she did something stupid like drool on herself, she averted her gaze and picked up the cake with hands that were a little too shaky for comfort.

She almost wished Simon would eat one of the other desserts, but he didn't. He accepted a hefty slice of her cake, and she found herself holding her breath as he took a bite. When he didn't say anything, she let the breath out slowly and tried to ignore the disappointment. She sliced off the end of her piece of pumpkin pie and listened to the various conversations going on around the table.

"It's delicious," Simon said beside her.

She looked up at the same time he glanced at her. "Thank you."

Their short interchange reminded her of a time when she, Simon and Carter had still been close. Carter and Simon had come into the bakery after school, the first day her mom had let her make something that could be offered to customers. It shook her to remember that had been a red velvet cake, too.

She lowered her gaze back to her pie. A smile tugged at her lips as she remembered what Simon had said about her cake that long-ago day.

"It's not awful." High praise from a middle-school-age boy.

Now, years later, Simon ate a second piece of her cake, and she tried not to let that mean so much to her. Tried to tell herself she was just latching onto anything positive in a month that had otherwise been horrible.

Hannah began fidgeting the way she always did when she was ready to get out of her high chair. Keri tossed her napkin next to her plate and picked Hannah up. When Hannah lay her little head against Keri's shoulder, her breath caught. She wanted so much to show this little motherless girl how much she loved her, but she couldn't trump the fear that she was asking for trouble if she let Hannah too far into her heart.

She glanced at Simon and realized she felt the same about everyone these days. Though she hadn't realized it until that moment, she'd pulled away from Sunshine, too. She didn't even feel like herself anymore.

"Can I hold her?" Hank asked as he stepped up next to Keri.

Hank had been good friends with her father, and seeing him again made her miss her dad more than she had in a long time. She ached that her parents had never known what it was like to be grandparents, to hold their first grandchild. But a part of her was almost glad they weren't there to experience the sorrow of burying their daughter.

"Keri?" Hank said.

"Oh, sure." She shook off the memories and handed Hannah over.

Hank's face lit up when he had her firmly in his arms. Hannah was like a little ball of sunshine, making people happy wherever she went. Keri, on the other hand, felt more like a thick, black cloud everyone would rather avoid. At least that's how people should feel around her.

Hoping some of her dark mood would dissipate, she started helping the other women clean the table. It wasn't a surprise to hear the TV come on, followed by the sound of football announcers.

"That girl is going to be a heartbreaker," Merline said as she nodded toward where Hannah sat on Hank's knee and Simon wiggled her bunny in her face, making her giggle.

"Yeah, she's already got all the men in the room wrapped around her tiny finger." Grace rubbed her pregnant belly. "I'm going to have to be careful or this bunch will spoil this one so rotten we won't be able to stand her."

"Have you picked out a name?" Keri asked.

"Olivia Rose."

"Rosie for short," Merline said as she patted Grace's belly with grandmotherly affection.

"That's a lovely name." Another memory from Sammi's pregnancy assaulted her. The two of them had been shopping for baby clothes and tossing potential names back and forth. They'd gotten progressively worse until the two of them were laughing so hard tears were streaming down their faces. Keri had feared Sammi might go into labor right there in the middle of the baby superstore. From the looks on the faces of the people working there, they'd been having the same kinds of thoughts.

God, how she missed her.

"Excuse me." It'd been years since she'd been down the hallway to the Teagues' guest bathroom, but she didn't have any trouble finding her way. She didn't have to go, just needed a couple of minutes alone to push sad thoughts away and figure out how quickly she could leave without being rude.

As she looked in the mirror, she saw the similarities between herself and Sammi. The same straight nose, same chin, same eyes. She closed her eyes to eclipse the image. For a couple of minutes, she stood and focused on doing no more than slowly breathing in and out. She'd get through this one day, one hour, one minute at a time.

Some sort of commotion from the living room caught her attention, and she figured the Cowboys must have scored. But the sound of Simon's voice calling her name sent her barreling out the door. Had something happened to Hannah? Had she tempted fate by trying to convince herself she would get through these trying days?

By the time she reached the living room, her heart was beating out of her chest. "What? What's wrong?"

"Nothing," Simon said, a smile stretched across his face. "We got Hannah to walk a couple of steps."

She focused on Hannah, who now sat on her bottom chewing on a plastic block. Tears pooled in Keri's eyes until everything around her grew blurry. If she'd thought she'd felt sorrow before, it was nothing compared to what exploded in her now. It'd been lurking, waiting to pounce. Without a word, she turned and almost ran out the back door.

Chapter Eight

Simon stared at Keri as she raced out of the house. The look that had been on her face—he'd never seen anything so sad in his life. In a moment of clarity, he understood his mistake.

"What?" Nathan said in confusion.

"It was Hannah's first steps, and she missed them." Simon stood, aware that everyone had gone quiet. He glanced at his mom, and she gave him a slight nod as though she knew what he was thinking. Chances were she did. She was uncanny that way.

He hesitated, thinking he was the last person Keri likely wanted to see, but he didn't want anyone else going after her, either.

When he stepped outside, he didn't see her. After a quick scan of the area, he figured she had to be in the barn. With a deep breath, he headed that way. He heard her sniffles as soon as he stepped inside the barn, but it took a couple of moments for his eyes to adjust enough to the dimmer light to see her. She stood at the far end of the barn, her shape a dark silhouette against the glow of the sunlight outside.

Again he considered whether he should approach her, but when he heard her take in a shaky breath it broke his heart. He closed the space between them. He could tell the moment she realized he was there because she stiffened.

"I'm sorry, Keri," he said. He wanted to touch her, try to somehow comfort her, but he feared that would just make things worse. "I shouldn't have said anything. Then you wouldn't have known you missed it."

Keri shook her head and turned a tear-stained face toward him. "It's not me who should have seen Hannah's first steps. Sammi should have been there. She should have been the one Hannah was walking to."

Not him. He felt as if he'd stolen something precious and there was no way to give it back.

Keri's hold on what little willpower she had crumbled, and a flood of tears poured from her eyes. "She should be here, not me. She shouldn't have died and left me all alone!"

Sobs overtook her, and Simon guided her into his arms. She tried to pull away, but he didn't let her.

"No," he said next to her ear. "It's time to let it all out."

And she did. She cried so hard that her entire body shook with the convulsions. Her hands knotted in the front of his shirt and tears soaked the fabric.

He rubbed his hand over her hair, smoothing it and trying to soothe her pain. When he felt about as helpless as he ever had, he planted a kiss on the top of her head. It was a testament to how much she was hurting that she didn't notice or comment on what he'd done.

"Why do they all leave me?" she asked, more vulnerable than he'd ever heard her.

He hugged her close. "I don't know."

She took a shuddering breath. "I...I'm afraid to love her, afraid she'll be taken away, too." She wiped at her tears. "Sometimes I think our family is cursed, that the

Mehlers fled Germany to escape it but brought it with them instead."

Simon leaned back just enough to look her in the eyes. He lifted one hand and wiped away tears with his thumb. "I don't think you're cursed. Sometimes life just sucks. But it eventually gets better."

"I'm not sure it'll get better this time. I think I'm all out of the ability to move past losing people."

He slid his hand to the side of her head, cupping her cheek and chin. "You underestimate yourself. You're the strongest person I've ever met."

She lowered her gaze to some point on the front of his shirt. "You don't know what it's like."

"You're right, I don't. Closest I've ever come is when my grandparents died and when we found out Ryan had been injured overseas. We had no idea how bad, if he'd live. But he did. And though it doesn't seem like it now, you're going to want to live again, too."

She looked up at him as if she didn't know who he was. To try to lighten the mood, he smiled and said, "Didn't know I moonlighted as a psychologist, did you?"

A little of the fire he equated with her flittered through her eyes. "God help your patients."

He let out a bark of laughter so loud that it spooked the horses nearest them. They snorted and sidestepped in their stalls.

"Why are you out here?" Keri asked, growing more serious.

He shrugged. "Because you looked like maybe you needed a shoulder to cry on."

"But we're not even friends anymore."

"I'm not so sure about that."

Her mouth parted, and he had to fight to keep from

lowering his lips to hers. Now wasn't the time. There might never be a time.

"I haven't exactly been nice to you," she said.

"No, but it's a nice change of pace from what I'm used to."

She smiled and swatted his arm. "You are way too full of yourself."

"I figure there are too many negative people in the world. It's my responsibility to be positive."

She rolled her eyes, and his heart lifted that her sorrow seemed to be abating, at least for the present. But before they shattered this moment, he had to say something.

"I can't tell you how sorry I am about Sammi. If I could bring her back for you, I would."

She wiped at another tear. "Thank you."

Again, she tried to pull away, but he only let her go a short distance and clasped her hands in his. "I know I'm not your favorite person, but I'd like to help you if you'll let me. We put aside what's past and just move forward."

He expected her to shoot him down in an instant, but she just stared at him without speaking for several seconds. He got the feeling a war was going on inside her—one side telling her to be practical and accept his help while the other clung to the old anger and tried to convince her that she didn't need help if it came from the likes of him. To his surprise, she finally nodded once. He knew how much that simple gesture cost her sense of self-sufficiency and pride.

Simon squeezed her hands in acknowledgment. "What do you say we go inside and see if we can coax a few more steps out of your niece?"

She appeared conflicted, and he knew she was combating her fear of caring.

"I know you've lost more people than anyone should, but it's not because you loved them."

She stood silent for several seconds, likely trying to decide if it was worth the risk, before agreeing. "Okay."

The surprises kept coming as she allowed him to hold one of her hands, but only as far as the barn's entryway. Once they stepped back into the bright light of day, she broke all contact. Even so, he felt as if they'd taken a huge step and started down an entirely different road together. He had no idea where that road might lead, but he was willing to find out.

AFTER A TRIP TO THE BANK the next week, Keri walked into the bakery office to find Simon playing patty-cake with Hannah. With mock annoyance, she crossed her arms and tapped her toe.

"I thought you were here to help get today's shipment ready."

Simon framed Hannah's chubby-cheeked face with his hand. "How am I supposed to resist this face?"

"Good grief, you're both besotted with each other." Keri turned and headed back to the kitchen as Sunshine returned from delivering a cake to the senior citizens center for a hundredth birthday party.

"How did Mr. Harlowe like his cake?"

"Got a good laugh out of it."

Keri had gotten a kick out of it, too, as she'd written "Happy 29th Birthday...for the 71st time" across the top of the cake.

"I hope I'm still that full of life at a hundred," Simon said as he wandered out of the office.

Sunshine laughed. "I can totally see that. You at the senior center, flirting with all the little old ladies."

"What, he does that now," Keri said.

"True."

"Hello, right here," Simon said.

That was how it'd been the past few days, the easy laughter and teasing. Sometimes it still didn't feel right to Keri, and guilt would well up in her like the tide coming ashore. She'd remind herself that he'd hidden the truth from her, that he hadn't tried harder to steer his best friend in the right direction. But she couldn't muster the same anger anymore. Truth was she didn't miss the tension and ugly feelings between Simon and her. Something had changed when he'd held her in his arms in the barn on Thanksgiving. She'd recognized part of the boy he'd once been, but there was more of the man he'd become. And while the boy might have done stupid and hurtful things, she sensed the man wouldn't.

If she were honest, it was nice having him around. He was good at keeping Hannah entertained, helped ease the load for her and Sunshine, even managed to drum up more business by convincing customers to buy more than they'd intended. She dreaded the day when he felt she didn't need his help anymore. Because he would leave, that she didn't doubt. He'd be distracted by police work, things on the ranch or a new woman to date. And she'd go back to just being someone he spoke to on the street.

"Penny for your thoughts," Simon said when he stepped up to the opposite side of the table and started assembling cake boxes.

"A whole penny? I'll have you know my thoughts are worth at least a dime."

"Oh, rich thoughts. Now I'm really curious."

She looked up and caught his gaze. Something about it made her heart trip. Since Thanksgiving, she'd relived the feel of him holding her way too many times. Those were dangerous thoughts to have. Though they might have set aside their past problems, at least for the time being, Simon Teague wasn't the kind of guy you fell for. Not if you wanted to keep your heart intact.

"Well, you can just stay curious." No way was she telling him she'd been daydreaming of how firm and warm his chest had felt against her cheek as she'd cried her heart out. Or how she'd never felt as safe as the moment when his arms had wrapped around her.

"Now, that sounds like a challenge. I'll find a way to get it out of you."

Keri ignored him and headed toward the front to help a customer. She made the mistake of making eye contact with Sunshine, and her friend gave her a knowing smile.

Throughout the afternoon, she kept Simon busy with tasks that kept him at least several paces away from her. She didn't want to be tempted to stare at him and give Sunshine more ammunition. If she didn't share how she was feeling about Simon with anyone, maybe it would be easier to ignore.

Yeah, right. If she didn't want to deal with those kind of feelings, she should kick him out of the bakery. But she didn't want to. When he was around, he inexplicably made her feel better. When she went home at night, having to care for Hannah in a house that felt emptier than it ever had, the loneliness nearly crushed her.

Midafternoon, Sunshine's son showed up after school about the time Erik stopped out front in the UPS truck. Sunshine directed Brett to help Simon and Erik load the boxes.

"So, what are you going to do about this infatuation that has been scorching the air in here all day?" Sunshine asked when all the guys were outside.

"You're imagining things." Keri continued filling out a supply order form without looking up.

"Nice try. But you can ask my optometrist. I've got twenty-twenty vision, and I've been seeing a lot of inter-ested glances being shot back and forth between you two."

Simon had been watching her? Her skin warmed at the thought, as if his gaze were roving over her at that moment.

She glanced out the front window to make sure Simon was still outside. "I'm not saying or doing anything."

"Why not?"

"I have too much else on my plate right now."

"You're afraid that boy will hurt you."

Keri completed the order form and set it to the side. "Chances are he would. You know how he is. He's not the sticking type."

"People change."

Keri met Sunshine's eyes. "Some people change, but not all of them."

Sunshine leaned back against the center worktable and crossed her arms. "I don't want to see you go through life alone, not when you've got so much to give someone."

Keri shook her head. "I'm not exactly the best catch in town. I'm surly, contrary, work all the time."

"And if you're aware of those things, you can change them. But I think you don't give yourself enough credit. You're loyal, a good friend, caring. You deserve to love someone and be loved back."

A laugh escaped Keri at that thought. "Do you hon-estly think Simon has the capacity to fall in love instead of repeated bouts of lust?"

"With the right woman, yes."

Sunshine seemed so sure that it startled Keri, leaving her speechless for a few moments.

"Well, that's all well and good if it happens, but I don't think I'm that woman."

Sunshine pushed away from the table as the guys came back in the front door. "That's where you're wrong."

Those words and all the possibilities that sprang from them kept reverberating in Keri's head the rest of the day, even when Simon had to go to the sheriff's department to take care of some of his own work. What would it be like being the woman who finally ended Simon's carefree dating ways?

No matter how much she tried, she couldn't imagine it for more than a couple of seconds.

After Sunshine and Brett left for the day, Keri fixed Hannah a new bottle and tickled her little feet until she giggled uncontrollably. Sometimes it still felt as if she was tempting fate by letting herself get closer and closer to Hannah, but her niece deserved to have someone love her fully and unconditionally. Keri wasn't Sammi, could never replace the mother Hannah lost, but she was going to do the best she could.

Across the street, she noticed Justine Ware putting up strings of Christmas lights around the front windows of her real estate office. With the Christmas in Blue Falls festivities the next day, she figured it was time to dig out her own decorations.

She pulled the ladder from behind the storage room door and positioned it next to the shelves that held the boxes of Christmas decorations. The two boxes of lights and decorations didn't prove any problem, but the tree was a different story. She could use another set of hands with the heavy and awkward box, but she really wanted to get the decorating done tonight. Tomorrow would be a busy day with festival preparations on top of her normal business.

When she had the box halfway off the shelf, she heard the front door open. "I'll be with you in a minute," she called out. The box got stuck on one of the shelf supports, so she leaned back to have room to pull it free. She gasped as her foot slipped off the ladder. She tried to grab something to break her fall, but her hands met with nothing but open air. Pain shot through her ankle as it got caught in the ladder and twisted a moment before she came to a jarring halt on the floor, the Christmas tree box on top of her.

"Keri?" Simon called as he rushed in the door. He dropped to the floor beside her and shoved the tree box off her. "What are you doing?"

"Wrestling with a big box?" She winced when she tried to move her ankle. "I think it won."

"Lord, woman, I leave you alone for two seconds and you take a header off a ladder."

"FYI, that wasn't in the plan."

He shook his head. "Can you stand?"

"Yeah, I think so." But when she tried, pain shot up her leg from her ankle. "Okay, maybe not."

Simon scooped her up into his arms.

"What are you doing?"

"Taking you to the hospital for an X-ray on that ankle. Maybe on your head, too."

"It's just sprained."

"Your ankle or your brain?"

She swatted him. "Put me down."

"Nope, I swore an oath to ensure the public safety, and you are part of the public."

"Simon."

"Don't argue. You won't win."

"But I don't close for another two hours."

He met her gaze, and her breath caught at how very close he was.

"I think the good people of Blue Falls can do without their sugar highs tonight."

"But—"

She got nothing else out because Simon lowered his mouth to hers and kissed her. After an initial jolt, she felt herself relax and lean into the kiss. The warmth of it, the soft feel of Simon's lips on hers, the sparks of electricity traveling outward from where they touched in a delicious cascade.

When he pulled away, he appeared as breathless as her. But then he smiled. "Well, that's one way to get you to stop talking."

With her brain scrambled and her heart beating fast, she couldn't manage to form a single word as Simon carried her outside and deposited her in the passenger seat of his truck.

"Hannah," she said, suddenly panicked.

"Don't worry. I'm going back to get her."

When he shut her door against the evening cold, she stared after him and raised her fingers to her lips. She still couldn't believe he'd kissed her. Maybe she'd hit her head when she fell and was out cold on the storage room floor.

But she doubted any dream could feel as real as what she was experiencing. Her entire body pulsed with heat and her nerve endings crackled. And she desperately wanted to kiss him again to see if the experience was really as good as she'd thought.

She dropped her hand to her lap when she saw Simon step outside the bakery with Hannah in her carrier and Keri's purse and keys. He sat Hannah down long enough to lock the front door then carried her to his side of the truck. When he opened the door, she heard him talking to Hannah.

"Yes, your aunt is clumsy, so we're taking a little trip to see the doc."

"I'm not clumsy," Keri said in self-defense.

"Is that right?" he said as he slid Hannah across the seat. "Back in a minute." He gave her a devilish grin, and her cheeks went critical with blushing.

She still hadn't managed to get it under control by the time he returned with the car seat base and hooked Hannah in safely. As he drove to the hospital, she occupied herself with checking Hannah's diaper and digging out her health insurance card.

"I'm going to feel like a fool going in there like this."

"Why?"

"Because it was stupid." It hit her then that she was going to have to be more careful from now on. She was the only person left for Hannah to depend on, and she couldn't stand the idea of her niece being left utterly alone if something happened to her, too.

"Come on," Simon said. "Don't beat yourself up over it. Accidents happen."

"Thought you said I was clumsy."

"Didn't say you were clumsy on purpose."

He managed to lighten her mood but not her resolve to be more careful in the future. No more antics that might lead to her breaking her neck.

When they reached the hospital, Simon ran inside and returned with a wheelchair.

"Yeah, this won't make me feel like a fool at all," she said as she got out of the truck and maneuvered into the chair.

"I could always carry you."

"I'll pass, thanks." Though the idea of another kiss made her wonder if perhaps she should accept his offer.

He pulled Hannah from her carrier and placed her in

Keri's lap. When he pushed them toward the emergency room door, Hannah giggled as though it was great fun.

"Hey, we ship your auntie off to X-ray and maybe I'll push you around the hospital," Simon said over Keri's shoulder to Hannah.

She clapped her little hands as if she understood and was all for that idea.

Though she'd hardly been apart from Hannah since she'd picked her up in Dallas, Keri trusted leaving her in Simon's care as she was rolled away to X-ray. Honestly, that kiss was occupying a lot more of her brainpower at the moment. Had it been just a way to get her to stop objecting to going to the hospital, or was there any way it could have meant something else? Could Simon be attracted to her the way she was to him? His touch had been tender Thanksgiving day, and he'd been spending a lot of time around the bakery when he didn't have to.

And friends didn't kiss like that, with desire wending its way around every nerve, every muscle, every organ in her body. Could she have been the only one to feel that?

"Good news, nothing broken," said Dr. Carrington when Keri was back in an examining room. "You did sprain it pretty good, and it's going to be purple for a few days. You need to keep it elevated as much as possible."

She looked at the young doctor, who'd definitely be a catch if her attractions didn't run in a different direction. Though he was a transplant from Houston, he'd been in Blue Falls long enough to know a lot of the locals, including her.

"Doc, you know this is the busy season for the bakery."

He tapped her knee with his clipboard. "Then I suggest you hire some help."

"Can you prescribe me some more money to do that?"

"Sorry, Keri. If I could do that, I'd prescribe it for

myself and be lounging on a warm beach with a nice cold one in my hand."

"Oh, I'll take some of that, too."

He laughed as he stood. "Seriously, it's going to hurt for a few days, and the more you can stay off of it, the faster it will heal."

She sighed but nodded.

After Dr. Carrington's nurse, Amanda Perkins, wrapped her ankle and gave her a set of crutches, Keri headed back toward the waiting room. She arrived just in time to see Simon go racing by with Hannah in the seat of a wheelchair. Her niece was giggling so hard that Keri couldn't help laughing, too.

Amanda walked up beside her.

"You got a psychiatric ward in this hospital?" Keri asked as she nodded toward Simon.

"Nope, sorry." Amanda laughed as Simon turned and headed back toward them. "Your niece is adorable." She nudged Keri's arm and gave her a meaningful smile. "Her chauffeur isn't bad, either."

As Simon reached them, Keri had to agree. Simon Teague just might be the sexiest man she'd ever laid eyes on.

"Come on, Hopalong," he said to her. "Let's get you home."

"Watch it," she said as she lifted a crutch. "I have weapons now."

He gave her a mischievous smile. "And I'm pretty sure I can outrun you."

She narrowed her eyes at him. "Just wait until I heal. I'll be able to catch your sorry butt then."

He picked up Hannah and pushed the empty wheelchair into an alcove with two others. "Maybe I'll let you."

Damn him if he didn't wink at her before turning around and heading toward the door outside.

In a flash, she thought of half a dozen things she could do to him when she caught him. And not one of them involved beating him with a metal crutch.

Chapter Nine

Simon listened as Keri thunked around the bedroom on her crutches, changing Hannah into her pajamas and giving her a freshly made bottle of milk. He'd offered to help, but she'd relegated him to her living room. Unable to sit still, he walked to the mantel and scanned the collection of framed family photos. Keri's parents on their wedding day. Her mom holding a newborn baby that he guessed was Sammi. Hannah in her red, white and blue outfit on the Fourth of July. Keri with Sammi and Carter, all in their basketball uniforms.

He paused when he reached Keri's prom picture. She'd gone with Adrian Stone, who was now an attorney in town. An irrational surge of jealousy made its presence known. Why, he had no idea. As far as he knew, Adrian and Keri hadn't dated since high school. And it wasn't as if Simon had laid claim to her.

Or had he? Though he'd admit to having thought about it, he'd been as surprised by their kiss earlier as she had been. Surprised it'd happened, surprised by how much he'd liked it and had wanted more.

He stared at the picture, at the shiny blue dress and fancy hairdo Keri had shown up in. She'd turned heads that hadn't expected to be turned by her. He even remembered her looking uncomfortable with the attention.

And she'd cured it by going back to the typical jeans-and-T-shirts Keri the next day.

The sound of the crutches on the wood floor drew his attention, but he didn't put the photo back on the mantel. Instead, he held it up facing her. "I wanted to ask you to dance that night."

She raised an eyebrow. "Probably a good thing you didn't."

Yeah, she'd still pretty much hated his guts at that point. He returned the photo to its designated spot.

"Hannah settled in for the night?" he asked.

"Yeah. I think all that wheelchair racing wore her out."

"It kept her entertained. I think everyone else waiting got a kick out of it, too."

And it'd kept him from examining too closely what was going on between him and Keri; why he'd felt the need to kiss her—

"Would you like some dinner?" she asked, and pivoted on her crutches toward the kitchen.

Someone knocked on the front door. "Got it covered," he said as he walked toward the door. He paid the teenager whose car idled in the driveway and accepted the pizza.

"You didn't have to do that," Keri said.

"Are you kidding? I'll use any excuse to eat Gia's pizza." He placed the box on the coffee table and motioned for her to sit down on the couch. "Come on, Gimpy. Time to put that foot up."

"Keep it up with the nicknames and you'll be wearing that pizza on your head."

He laughed as he crossed to the kitchen for napkins and drinks. As he stared into the refrigerator, he noticed lots of fresh fruit, bottles of water and a jug of milk. "You not have any beer?" he called.

"No, I've got a baby in the house."

He leaned around the doorway separating the two rooms. "What, you think she's going to toddle in and pop a cold one?"

She stuck her tongue out at him, and it was so like old times between them that he couldn't help but smile widely back at her.

"There are sodas in one of the bottom drawers."

Plates, napkins and drinks in hand, he returned to the living room. She might argue that she was okay, but he noticed she'd propped her foot on a cushion from the nearby chair.

"How's your ankle?"

"Fine." She hesitated a moment. "Actually, it aches like the dickens." She reached into her purse and pulled out a bottle of medicine, no doubt painkillers. "Guess it's time for one of these. Hope they don't make me loopy."

"Oh, now that might be fun."

He placed two pieces of the pepperoni pizza on a plate and handed it to her, then snatched up the remote control and turned on the TV. After a couple of clicks, he found the Spurs-Lakers game.

"Hope they play better tonight than they did against the Jazz the other night," she said. "They couldn't hit the basket if their lives depended on it."

As they ate, Simon marveled at how easy it felt between them now. He knew if he pointed it out, she'd do something like kick him out of the house, so he kept his thoughts to himself. He had to chuckle when Keri got carried away telling the refs they were blind or fist pumping when the Spurs made a tough shot. A couple of times she had to rein in her enthusiasm or risk waking Hannah.

If there was one thing other than the bakery and Hannah that Keri was passionate about, it was basketball.

"Do you ever miss playing?" he asked when the game went to halftime.

"Yeah. I go to the games out at the high school when I can, but sometimes I itch to take to the court again. Can't say I miss running drills, though. Or shin splints."

She leaned back against the couch and wiggled the toes on her injured foot then winced. "I can't imagine a worse time for me to injure myself. We'll have two to three times the traffic in the bakery tomorrow."

"I wouldn't worry about it."

"Easy for you to say. You won't have eager shoppers popping in the sheriff's department all day long."

Already, a plan was forming in his mind, but he didn't dare put it into motion until she was asleep. Which, he realized, might not be too long. Keri had gone quiet and closed her eyes. She wasn't asleep yet, but she was getting closer with every breath. He eyed her lips, wondering what she'd do if he kissed her again.

When her breathing changed, indicating she was asleep, he pulled out his phone and sent a couple of text messages. Less than a minute later, he got the answers and smiled.

Keri jerked awake beside him, and he could tell from the pained look on her face that she'd had a bad dream. She looked around disoriented. The overwhelming need to soothe her took over and he wrapped his arm around her and pulled her to his side.

"I need to go to bed," she said a bit sluggishly. Tiredness and the pain medication were joining forces to tug her toward sleep again.

"Shh, come here," he said. He slid against the end of the couch and leaned back, taking her with him. When she stretched her legs out, he grabbed the quilt off the back of the couch and covered her with it.

He wasn't going anywhere, and if he was honest, he'd rather have her in his arms than in another room.

She drifted off again and cuddled closer to him, laying her head against his chest. He sucked in a breath when she brushed against sensitive areas that suddenly had an idea that had nothing to do with sleep.

Maybe this sleeping arrangement hadn't been the best idea, after all.

KERI SNUGGLED CLOSER against the warmth of her pillow, trying to hang on to the dream of Simon kissing her all over her body. Every single nerve ending tingled in the most delicious way, and she hated when wakefulness started to steal pieces of the dream, making it seem less real.

Another truth made her freeze. She wasn't lying on a pillow. It was too hard and moved up and down in the distinct rhythm of human breathing. She assessed her position and found it right up there on the embarrassment scale. Her hip pressed against a part of Simon that seemed happy to see her.

Her face flaming, she tried to extricate herself. But when she raised her head from his chest, she found his eyes open and looking at her.

"Good morning," he said with a hint of teasing.

"Hi." Wow, she felt really dumb in that moment. If she found out she'd been either talking or moaning in her sleep, she was just going to die of mortification.

"You seemed to sleep well."

"I doubt you did."

"I don't know," he said. "Can't say I mind waking up with a pretty woman on top of me."

She tried to push herself up and away, but he stopped

her retreat by wrapping his strong arms around her back and pulling her down to his chest.

"What are you doing?" she asked, hating how breathless she sounded.

"This." All protests died when he kissed her again, long and very, very thorough.

Somehow she found the will to push away. "We can't do this."

"Why not?" He sounded distinctly out of breath, which caused her entire body to flush with need.

"Because I have to get to work for one."

"No, you don't."

"Simon, the Christmas festivities are today."

"And this time, you'll get to enjoy them because you're not working."

"Sunshine can't do everything by herself."

"She won't have to. You have a long list of volunteers who will be manning the fort today."

She stared at him, wondering who this guy inhabiting Simon's body was. Though it was difficult to relinquish her control, she had to admit she liked the thought of not having to hobble around the bakery all day.

"Thank you."

He offered her a self-satisfied smile. "Go ahead, tell me how awesome I am."

She gave in to a wicked streak and showed him instead, capturing his mouth in what was supposed to be a quick kiss. But as soon as their lips touched, Simon moaned and rolled her onto her back, deepening the kiss in the process.

Those all-over tingles she'd experienced in the dream came back. Only this time they were real and threatened to set her skin on fire. Simon cupped the back of her head and used his tongue to turn her mind to mush.

When he broke the kiss, her heart was hammering. "What are we doing?"

"I thought that much was obvious," he said against her lips.

"But…" She lost her train of thought when his hand started making its way up her rib cage. The only crazy thought that made it through the haze of desire Simon was stoking in her was that she hated the fabric of her shirt. It was preventing his palm from touching her skin.

"Stop thinking," he said. "For once, Keri, just let go."

When his thumb skimmed the edge of her breast, letting go sounded like a really good idea. She reached up and ran her fingers through his hair, pulling him down to where she could kiss him.

His lips left hers and started an exploratory journey along her cheek, across her ear and down her neck.

"I've lost my mind," she said as she searched for breath.

Simon's lips came back to her ear and whispered, "I think I like when you lose your mind." He nipped her ear with his teeth at the same time his big hands found their way underneath her shirt.

Keri held her breath as all of her attention focused on the feel of his palms moving across her stomach and ribs. Hot and rough-textured, but in a delectable, "send sparks through your entire body" way. Desperate for more of him, she managed to get her hands to the buttons on the front of his shirt. She didn't let go of his mouth as she worked the buttons free only to find a T-shirt underneath. Frustrated, she gripped the bottom of the T and pulled upward.

Simon laughed against her mouth. "Impatient, are we?"

"Shut up and take it off."

"Yes, ma'am."

When he pulled the shirt over his head and revealed his well-toned torso, she'd swear her mouth watered.

Simon's mouth quirked into a crooked grin. "Like what you see?"

Oh, God, yes.

"It'll do in a pinch."

Challenge flared to life in his eyes as his hands made a sudden movement, bringing them back under her shirt, then under the confines of her bra. Before she could speak, he'd captured her mouth again and had unfastened the bra's clasp as though he'd done it a thousand times before.

He probably had, on other women. Common sense tried to take hold, but Simon banished it the moment he pushed her shirt up and his mouth latched onto her right breast.

She nearly bucked right off the couch, which only gave him better access and increased the pressure building deep inside of her. She wanted this man, all of him. His heart and soul might take some doing, but he seemed more than willing to give her his body. And her body was thinking along the same lines.

A flicking motion of his tongue against her breast had her gasping and digging her fingers into his back. When his mouth moved to the other breast as though he didn't want it to feel left out, she thought she'd never imagined such a sensation, as if every muscle was taut and on the verge of snapping.

When she let her hands roam to the front of his jeans and slid her fingers below the waist, Simon's body jerked. And in that moment, his natural teasing disappeared and he seemed to become as desperate for her as she was for him. The thrill that shot through Keri had her at work on the button fastening his jeans. She pushed all possible repercussions from her mind, leaving only room for pure sensation and the tremendous desire to have this man inside her.

It took a moment for the sound beyond them to penetrate her fog of lust, but when it did she stopped her exploration. Hannah was crying in the bedroom.

"Pretend you don't hear that," Simon said next to her neck, sounding a little desperate.

"I have to go to her." She would not let Hannah cry with hunger or a wet diaper while she went wild and crazy on the couch.

Simon dropped next to her and groaned his frustration. When she tried to rise, he gently placed his arm across her chest. "I'll go."

She didn't argue, but that was likely because he'd just scrambled her brain like a skillet of eggs. Once he was on his feet and headed toward the bedroom, she couldn't take her eyes off the play of muscles in his back and the way his jeans hung on his narrow hips. Merciful heavens, that man was made for sex. No wonder he was so danged popular with every female who crossed his path. He was a male version of a siren in a cowboy hat and sexy-as-hell jeans.

When he disappeared into her bedroom, she sat up, fastened her bra and pulled her shirt closed, marveling at how easily and quickly she'd taken leave of her senses. She'd just about had hot sex with the hottest guy in town, maybe in Texas. A guy she'd been angry with for years.

How in the world was she ever going to be able to look him in the eye again without imagining him naked and driving her toward an earth-shattering climax? She lifted her palms to her flaming cheeks. She couldn't go anywhere until she got that under control. One look and Sunshine would know something hot and sweaty had happened between her and Simon. Heck, the whole town would probably be able to read it on her face like a bill-board.

She'd just gotten her shirt buttoned and smoothed her hair when Simon popped his head out of the bedroom. "Somebody is in dire need of new drawers." He made a playful wave of his hand past his nose, making her laugh.

Thankful for the distraction, she stood and grabbed her crutches. When she reached the doorway leading into the bedroom, he didn't move, forcing her to edge past him, breathing in his musky male scent and wishing he'd put on a shirt before she jumped his bones right there.

When she glanced up at him, his smile told her he knew exactly what he was doing.

"You are evil," she said.

He laughed and wandered out to the living room.

She closed the bedroom door behind her and leaned against it, trying to bring her heartbeat under control. When she looked at Hannah, her niece wasn't crying any-more but didn't look particularly happy, either. Keri shook her head slowly back and forth against the door.

"What have I gotten myself into, Hannah?"

Unfortunately, Hannah didn't have any answers.

THE LAST THING SIMON wanted to do was go to work pa-trolling the crowd filling Blue Falls. He wanted to grab Keri, whisk her back to her house and finish what they'd started. It was no secret he'd dated his fair share of women, but none of them had turned on the switch in him that Keri had. It'd freaked him out and driven him to consume her at the same time.

Even after he dropped her and Hannah off at the bakery and returned to his apartment, he hadn't been able to get the feel of her under his hands off his mind. The smell of her simple, fruity shampoo out of his nose. The taste of her off of his tongue. He paused in putting on his uniform and cursed. He had to stop thinking about her or he wasn't going to be able to go out in public. Not even the cold shower he'd just taken seemed to do the trick.

He shook his head as he went out the door. No other woman had ever affected him this way. He'd always been casual about dating, steering clear of anything too serious. But the word *mine* had blazed to life in his head as he'd held Keri earlier. The thought of her being that way with anyone else drove him a little mad.

What the hell was happening to him? After all the teasing he'd shot toward Nathan and Ryan, was their need to commit to one woman rubbing off on him?

No, couldn't be.

Could it?

He'd better hope not because he wouldn't be surprised if Keri was already mapping out a plan to boot him out of her life again.

But she hadn't seemed unwilling to be with him that morning. In fact, she'd looked as hungry as he'd felt.

He deliberately started out at the opposite end of town from the bakery. Maybe by the time he'd walked the entire length of Main Street he'd be thinking like himself again. Or maybe he'd send Jack or Pete to watch things on that end.

By the time he'd popped into half a dozen businesses to say hello, given directions to three groups of tourists, done a double take at the pair of camels that had to be bound for the live nativity and bought a cup of hot chocolate at the high school band's booth, the urge to see Keri had grown instead of dissipated.

Before he did something stupid like barge into the bakery and carry her off to that little office of hers, he retraced his steps to his patrol vehicle and drove past all the shops and restaurants that rimmed the lake. All looked peaceful, and judging by the number of cars, people were in a buying mood. He should get going on his own shopping soon.

He was usually a gift card kind of guy, but he'd found it fun to buy Evan actual presents for his birthday. Building sets, Avengers action figures and a new pair of cowboy boots for his growing feet.

And his new niece couldn't come into this world without a pile of presents from her uncle Simon. Dolls and stuffed animals and little frilly dresses.

Maybe he could get Hannah something, too.

And Keri.

He rubbed his hand over his face. That woman had gotten under his skin, into his blood. He couldn't remember ever wanting a woman as much as he wanted her. The difference in how he felt toward her made him squirm in his seat.

Man, he needed to get his mind on something else. He swung into the parking lot for his mom's art gallery.

"Hey, Simon," Grace said when he walked in. "Can't say I expected to see you here today."

When he met her eyes, he saw a mischievous twinkle and groaned inwardly. He couldn't do anything in this town without someone noticing. Normally, it didn't matter, but for some reason he didn't want people whispering about Keri as if she was one of his purported conquests. She…she was more than that. Not that half the tales about him were true, anyway. He just never corrected anyone. Now he wished he had.

"You okay?" Grace said.

"Other than everyone knowing my business, sure. Fantastic."

"You had to know people would figure it out when you rallied the troops last night."

"I was trying to help Keri out. She can't even walk on both feet. How was she supposed to work today?"

At least helping out a friend was what he'd told himself he was doing when he'd texted Sunshine and his mom to help scrounge up enough extra hands to take shifts at the bakery today.

He nodded toward where his mom was busy talking to gallery visitors. "I can only imagine what she's thinking."

"Pretty sure she'd already have the wedding cake ordered if Keri wasn't the wedding cake queen of Blue Falls."

He groaned again and shook his head. "She must have dropped me on my head when I was a baby."

"Aw, come on," Grace said. "I think it's great."

"Really? Why?"

The question seemed to surprise her. "Why wouldn't I?"

He leaned on the front counter opposite his sister-in-law. "Because it's all kinds of complicated, and I don't do complicated."

"Maybe you've just maxed out on easy and it's time for something different."

He made a sound like he wasn't so sure about that.

"Do you like her?"

"Yes."

"Really like her?"

He hesitated and realized how much time he'd spent with Keri lately. How often he'd thought and dreamed about her when they weren't together. "Yeah. Though it makes no sense."

"Why not?"

"We've known each other forever, the last few years of which she's hated me."

"Maybe it wasn't hate but hurt."

He considered that, wondered.

"Besides, it wouldn't be the first time a man in this family fell for a woman that logic said he shouldn't," Grace said.

"Remind me to beat up my brothers for setting that precedent."

Grace laughed and touched her rounded belly, perhaps unconsciously.

"You might like to avoid complicated relationships, but I'm here to tell you that they're worth it. And Brooke would tell you the same thing."

His instinct might be telling him to get out while the getting was good, but damned if his heart wasn't telling him something else entirely. And despite how he teased Nathan and Ryan about their old ball and chains, he now realized some previously unawakened part of him was jealous of what they had. There was no denying he'd never seen them happier.

Question was, could he change who he was and try something serious?

Or was what he'd been until now a lie? Maybe steps to becoming who he was supposed to be, with the woman he was supposed to be with?

Only one way to find out.

Chapter Ten

"I can't believe he did all this." Keri eyed the decorations around the bakery for what had to be the hundredth time. The Christmas tree she'd tried unsuccessfully to extricate from the storage room stood next to the front window, fully decorated and sparkling with lights. Garland and white lights hung from the front counter. Her mom's collection of Santas sat along the top of the display case, and Christmas carols played on the CD player.

"If I didn't know better, I'd say that boy was smitten," Sunshine said as she replenished the supply of sprinkle-covered sugar cookies on the table that also held the coffee urn and hot cider.

When they'd left her house that morning, Keri was jaded enough to think that maybe Simon had been nice to her lately so he could get into her pants. Because maybe he'd exhausted all other datable women in Blue Falls, or he saw the woman who'd harbored an ugly anger toward him as a challenge.

But all those thoughts had evaporated the moment she'd stepped into the bakery and seen its transformation. Somehow Simon had pulled together enough volunteers to decorate the bakery, help Sunshine with the preparations for the day's festivities and man the store in one-hour shifts. There had even been instructions left for her— "Stay off your ankle. Sheriff's orders."

"Do you really think that's possible, after everything that's happened between us? I mean, I've not exactly been nice to him."

Sunshine came to stand beside where Keri sat on a stool at the cash register. "You tell me. You think he would have gone through all this trouble for just anyone? Come to the bakery all those times to help out? Lent a hand with Hannah?" Sunshine paused until Keri met her gaze. "Face it. He's not the same person he was when your friendship ended."

Keri knew Sunshine was right. But how did Simon and she just turn off the past as if it'd never happened?

Sunshine rested her hand atop Keri's. "You grab that sexy hunk of a man and you don't let go, you hear me?"

A smile started in her mind and spread to the edges of her mouth, tugging until it'd consumed her lips and quite possibly the rest of her face. Sunshine smiled back.

"Glad to see you're on board," her friend said. She glanced around as the front door opened yet again. "Speak of the devil."

Keri's heart started racing at the sight of Simon filling the doorway. She'd seen him in his uniform a million times around town, but something about how he looked in it today made her mouth water. What was it about a man in uniform that made women's hormones stand up and tap dance? Maybe it was because she knew what a magnificent chest and arms lay beneath that shirt and badge.

She smiled at him, and he seemed surprised for a moment before he sauntered toward her, grabbing a sugar cookie along the way.

"I thought you might toss me out on my head when you saw me," he said low so no one else could hear.

"Are you kidding? I'm living like a queen on my throne today thanks to you."

He laughed, but some emotion flitted across his face so quickly she couldn't identify it. Still, it nagged at her and the idea that she shouldn't tease at that moment somehow formed in her mind.

"Seriously, thank you," she said.

When he met her eyes, there was a very different Simon Teague looking at her, one who seemed older and more serious. Like a younger version of his father.

"What would you say if I asked you to go out with me?"

Her heart leaped so powerfully it nearly knocked her off the stool. Heat whooshed throughout her body. But she tried to play it cool. After all, the bakery was full of people enjoying refreshments and conversations about everything from what they'd bought so far to who they thought was going to be crowned Blue Falls's Christmas Queen.

"I'd say yes."

Again with the surprise on his face. It was so out of character for him that she had to laugh a little.

"What's so funny?"

"Nothing."

He leaned closer and whispered, "I'll think of some way to get it out of you."

Her face went inferno hot when she glanced past him and saw Sunshine and Anne Marie Wallace each giving her two thumbs-up.

"When we don't have an audience," Simon added, which only made her face grow hotter.

He took a bite of his cookie, winked at her and took a step away. "Well, back to protecting the good folks of Blue Falls."

As he left, Keri knew she had a stupid grin on her face, and she didn't care who saw it.

The afternoon was filled with an increasing number of shoppers. The locals had come out in droves for the annual Christmas parade and lighting of the town's Christmas tree. Tourists flocked to town for special sales in the popular shops and a taste of a small-town Christmas.

A tinge of sadness crept into Keri's heart. Sammi had always loved coming back for this, had looked forward to sharing it with Hannah. Keri pulled herself up straight, determined to give Hannah what her mother wasn't able to—her first Christmas in Blue Falls experience.

As if Sunshine had been reading her mind, she came out of the office with Hannah dressed in a little Santa suit complete with hat.

Keri laughed. "Where did that come from?"

"I couldn't resist when I saw it. Isn't it adorable?"

"It is." Keri accepted her niece from Sunshine. "Aren't you just the cutest Christmas baby ever?"

"Never seen cuter." The familiarity of the male voice froze Keri for a moment.

Keri turned with Hannah in her arms and stared into her brother's eyes. "Carter."

"Hey, it's two of my favorite ladies," he said as he rounded the end of the display case.

Keri felt as if she'd been hit by lightning and her feet had melted to the floor. She'd thought she'd be glad to see him, and part of her was. But loss and anger crashed into her until she started shaking.

"Trying to teach Hannah the family business already?"

It made Keri furious that he'd marched right into the bakery without an "I'm sorry for disappearing" or "Wow, how I've missed you." And he acted like he and Hannah were the best of friends. He didn't even know her, had seen her once in her life when she was barely a month old.

Keri took a deliberate step back, wincing as she accidentally put pressure on her ankle, and her action didn't go unnoticed by her brother.

"What's wrong, Keri?"

A painful lump grew in her throat. As if Sunshine could read what she was thinking, she extended her arms and took Hannah. Keri marshaled enough energy to grab her crutches and stomp toward the back door. She didn't say anything as Carter followed her.

"What happened to your ankle?"

She didn't answer him.

"What's going on?" he asked when the door closed behind them. "You're freaking me out."

Keri rounded on him. "Where have you been? I've called you a million times and the number doesn't work."

He lowered his eyes. "Sorry about that. I lost my job and let the phone go."

She threw up her hands. "God, Carter. When are you going to grow up?"

"Why are you so mad? It's not the first time I've gone without a phone."

Hot tears burned her eyes. "But it's the first time your sister died!"

Carter just stared at her, as if she'd been speaking in a language he didn't understand. "What?"

Keri hugged herself against the December chill. "Last month, Sammi and Ben died in a car wreck."

He glanced toward the back door of the bakery as if he could see Hannah on the other side, then stumbled over to collapse atop the hood of her car.

"What…" He cleared his throat, having evidently developed a lump to match hers. "What happened?"

"Their car flipped during an ice storm." She looked up at the sky. She thought it should be gray and turbulent like her feelings, but it mocked her with its blue, sunny cheer. "I needed you, and you were nowhere to be found."

Carter stared at the ground between his feet. "I can't believe it."

She knew that feeling well. She lived it day in and day out. Though she had her bright moments, there were still plenty of dark ones, too. Ones when she felt as if the truth was stabbing her in the heart and twisting.

He looked up and met her eyes with his watery ones. "I'm so sorry, Keri. I would have been here if I'd known."

"But you weren't. Thankfully, not everyone is as irresponsible as you."

He jerked as if he'd been slapped. Good. It was time he really thought about how his actions had consequences.

Simon may have made mistakes in the past, but he didn't run away from his family and his duty to them. Even though he was the sheriff, he still put in hours of work on the ranch, too. He even took on responsibilities that weren't his to bear. Like boxing up cakes and babysitting a motherless child.

"Why did you come back?" she asked. She'd ignored how he always strolled into town when he needed something, hadn't wanted to believe that about her brother. But now the truth stood out like a huge neon sign in the nighttime desert.

Carter sat for long moments without saying anything. She imagined he wanted to deny it, but something about the look on her face and her tone told him to not even try.

"I need a job."

"Then get one."

He looked up at her, but she ignored the shame in his

eyes, not trusting herself to judge whether it was real or not.

"I was hoping I could work here."

"No."

"Keri, please. I'm desperate."

"Why? Are you in some kind of trouble?"

"No."

Her heart broke that she didn't believe him.

"I swear to you, I've changed," he said.

"Now, where have I heard that before?"

He eyed her like he didn't know her. "When did you get so harsh?"

"When I was left alone to run our family's business, keep up our family's house and raise our sister's daughter."

"But that's what I'm saying. I can help with all that. I want to."

She fought against the old urge to blindly trust him. "Sure, you might stay for a little while, but you'll eventually leave. You always do."

"No, I swear it."

Oh, how she wanted to believe him, to have the remnants of her family together in one place. But she somehow found the strength to stick with her refusal.

"If you want to stay in Blue Falls and work, you're going to have to find a job somewhere else." She swallowed before pressing on. "And you can't stay at the house."

"You're going to make me sleep in my car?"

"You need to learn some responsibility, Carter."

"I have!"

"Then prove it." Before she broke down and cried in front of him, she left him standing in the alley and went back into the bakery.

Once inside, she leaned against the door and shut her eyes. And prayed she hadn't just made a huge mistake.

SIMON CRUISED DOWN Lakeshore Drive, his thoughts more on the fact Keri had consented to go out with him than making sure all was well with the hordes of shoppers. Still he did a double take as he passed Gia's Pizza. He hit the brakes and pulled into the edge of the parking lot.

"I'll be damned," he said as he stared out the windshield at Carter Mehler in the flesh. He'd run every check he could think of and always seemed to be a step behind Carter. And now here he was. He slipped out of the SUV and walked around to the front. "Carter."

His former best friend looked up, and for a moment he seemed poised halfway between running and standing his ground.

"Hey, Simon."

"When did you get into town?"

"Why? Am I on the Blue Falls watch list?"

"Do you need to be?"

Carter leaned back against his car, his arms crossed. Simon noticed how tired and haggard he looked.

"I don't need the third degree today, okay?"

"You've seen Keri."

Carter nodded as though it took all his energy.

They may have had their differences, but Simon wasn't heartless. "I'm sorry about Sammi and Ben."

Carter stared down at the asphalt. "I keep thinking I'll wake up and it won't be true."

He'd heard Keri say much the same thing, had felt it himself. Seeing Carter so soon after he found out the news made it fresh and raw again. God, how must Keri be feeling right now? When he'd left the bakery earlier, she'd been smiling and finally happy. He tried not to hate Carter for likely ruining that.

"I feel like I've lost both sisters today," Carter said, his shoulders slumping. "Keri's mad at me, and I deserve it. I've got to make it up to her."

"That's going to take some doing."

"I know." Carter looked back at the pizzeria. "I don't even have time to grieve. I've got to find a job."

Had he asked Keri for one? Had she turned him down? He knew that would be hard for her, but it told him that maybe she really had believed him the other day.

"Then you're staying?"

"I want to. I've just… I've got to find work." Carter's words and posture held a desperation Simon didn't like. If he was in some sort of trouble and he brought it to Keri's doorstep, Simon would be hard-pressed not to toss him out of town on his head. That or throw him in a cell.

"Your sister doesn't need anything else to worry about. She's been through enough the past month."

Carter looked at him with questions in his eyes. He probably wondered about the unexpected familiarity in Simon's words. Well, let him wonder. What was between Keri and him was none of Carter's business.

He just hoped there still was something between Keri and him.

"I know," Carter finally said. "I will make it up to her."

"I'm going to hold you to that."

Carter gave him a curious look. "Am I missing something?"

Simon walked back to the driver's side door of his vehicle. "You've missed a lot, Carter. A whole hell of a lot."

"CAN I GET YOU ANYTHING else?" Sunshine asked as she placed a cup of coffee on the table next to the bakery's front window.

"No, I'm fine," Keri said. At least as fine as she could be now that her world had been turned upside down yet again. She alternated between being proud of how she'd stood up to Carter and wanting to race after him, pull him into her arms.

"For what it's worth, I think you did the right thing. People have to grow up sometime, and enabling them to do the exact opposite isn't doing them any favors."

"I know."

"But it doesn't make it any easier."

Keri gave her best friend a sad smile and shook her head. "No, it doesn't."

When the front door opened, Simon's tall frame filled the entire entrance. She knew the moment she met his eyes that he'd heard about Carter being back in town.

Sunshine patted her on the shoulder then disappeared into the office. After a moment, Keri heard her engaging in baby talk with Hannah.

"Guess you heard who just blew back into town," she said.

"Saw him, actually."

"Where?"

"Outside Gia's."

She nodded. "No doubt putting in a job application. I hear he's been to at least a dozen places in town this afternoon."

Simon slid into the chair opposite her and took her hands in his. "I'm proud of you."

"I am, too, but my heart also hurts like it's been stomped on."

"Maybe he'll surprise us this time."

She suspected he doubted Carter had changed, but she appreciated him trying to give her something to hope for.

She didn't say whether she believed one way or the

other because she didn't know. Instead, she just stared out the window at the comings and goings of her neighbors and the visitors to town.

"Don't let him tear you apart, Keri. You deserve to be happy."

She looked across the table at Simon. Yes, she did deserve that, and she wanted to be happy with him. She forced a smile. Today, she was going to enjoy the festivities as she'd planned. There'd be plenty of time to dwell on her brother's misguided traipsing through life tomorrow.

A glance at the clock revealed that more time had passed than she'd thought. "You better go. They can't start the parade without you."

He hesitated as if he might blow it off.

"I'll make sure Hannah sees you." The indication that she was going to watch the parade was what finally prompted him to move.

He squeezed her hand before standing. "See you later?"

She nodded.

Evidently satisfied, he put his hat back on and headed out to perform his holiday duty. Keri stared down the street long after Simon disappeared, until Sunshine returned with a bundled-up Hannah.

"Look who's ready to see Santa Claus." Sunshine tickled Hannah, making her giggle.

Keri's eyes filled with tears, but she blinked them away. She would mourn her sister for the rest of her days and had no idea if Carter would straighten out his life. But today needed to be all about happiness and fun. Though she might not remember it, Hannah's first Christmas wasn't going to be full of tears and sadness.

When the three of them walked out the door, she noticed that Ryan and Brooke had parked right in front of the bakery in the end parking space and lowered the tailgate of Ryan's truck. Brooke patted the area beside her.

"We saved you a spot over here where Hannah can see everything," she said.

Simon really had thought of everything.

She slid onto the tailgate and propped the crutches against it before extending her arms to take Hannah from Sunshine.

"Hey, sweetie pie," Brooke said as she caressed Hannah's cheek. "You are just the prettiest little girl."

She really was, and a burst of love for her niece nearly had Keri in tears again.

"How's your ankle?" Brooke asked, distracting her.

"Throbs a lot, but I think it's my pride that suffered more."

"I wouldn't worry about it." She leaned close, away from Ryan. "It does these guys' egos good to let them think they're rescuing damsels in distress now and again."

Keri admired Brooke for being able to laugh about it when Ryan actually had helped rescue her from an abusive ex-boyfriend several months ago. He really was a hero, twice over if you considered he'd served in the Army, too.

But was Simon any less a hero? Not to her. From the moment he'd ushered her to Dallas and stayed by her side as she'd had to identify Sammi's body and take custody of Hannah, he'd been watching out for her. Even when she hadn't wanted him there, had made that clear to him, he'd stuck around. Sure, he cloaked a lot of it in teasing and flirting, but that was just who he was and she was thankful for everything just the same.

The blare of a siren caused everyone to jump, and Hannah screwed up her face as if she might cry.

"It's okay, honey," Keri said, and turned Hannah

around on her lap to face the street. "Look, it's just the parade starting."

As the sheriff's department vehicle drew close, Keri's heart leaped to attention. It proved difficult not to smile like a fool as Simon drove closer, leading the parade. When he came close enough, she leaned down next to Hannah's ear.

"Look, Hannah, it's Simon." She took Hannah's little hand and waved it at him.

He saw them and waved back, giving Hannah a wide smile. Then his gaze shifted to Keri and held for a long moment. She felt the intensity of that stare all over her body as if he was actually touching her.

Wow, the imagination was a powerful thing.

The only reason she sat through the rest of the parade was because Hannah seemed to be captivated by everything that went by—marching band, cowboys and cowgirls on horses, carolers decked out in their Dickensian finest, floats from which people threw candy and, finally, Santa Claus riding on the town's biggest fire truck.

"If you're a good girl, he will bring you lots of presents," Keri said as she hugged Hannah close.

By the time the fire truck passed, Keri realized how cold it'd grown and was ready to go back inside for some hot cider and cookies. Sunshine had already gone back to the bakery to prepare for the afterparade crowd and the final shoppers before the stores closed and everyone migrated to city hall for the Christmas tree lighting.

"I'll take her," Brooke said as she scooped Hannah into her arms.

When Keri noticed how Brooke was looking at Hannah, she wondered how long it would be before she and Ryan started their own family.

The bakery got so busy after the parade that Keri

didn't have much time to think about Simon, but she still looked up in anticipation each time the front door opened to admit more people.

Once she saw Carter across the street watching the bakery, and she had to fight her instinct to forgive him for everything and invite him fully into her life again. But she had Hannah to think of now, and her niece needed positive role models. People like Simon.

How much her opinion of him had changed.

"These are delicious," a woman said as she sampled a lemon cupcake. "I'll take a dozen of them."

With both Sunshine and Brooke busy helping other people, Keri hopped off the stool and hobbled without her crutches to the display case. She managed to pull out a box and start filling it with cupcakes.

"Let me finish that."

She looked up into Simon's face. Where had he come from?

"You aren't supposed to be on that foot. Back to the stool before I carry you over there."

She did her best to look annoyed with him, but she ended up having to bite her bottom lip to keep from smiling. In fact, it proved impossible to keep her smile at bay during the next hour as Simon made conversation with the milling customers and sent her glances across the room.

Finally, everyone began filtering out to the lighting ceremony.

"You go on," Sunshine said when Keri started to do the nightly reconciliation and bank deposit.

"I can finish."

"I know you can, but you're not going to. Now shoo."

Another part of Keri awakened, a part she'd unconsciously shut off after Sammi's death, and she pulled Sunshine into her arms for a hug. "Thank you for always being there."

"Where else would I be, silly? If I made this many cinnamon rolls at home, I'd be as big as the Alamodome."

"I'm serious."

"I know. Now go."

As Keri put on her coat and reached for her crutches, Simon retrieved Hannah and effortlessly placed her on his shoulders.

"Oh, God, don't drop her." Keri reached toward Hannah as if to catch her.

"Don't worry. I've got her."

She trusted him, really she did. But as they walked toward the park surrounding city hall, Hannah's position still made her nervous. When they reached the park, Simon booted a couple of smooching teenagers off one of the benches so Keri could sit.

"Hannah, I know you like being up there, but I think I make your auntie nervous." In a big flourish and spin that made Hannah laugh her infectious laugh, he removed her from his shoulders and placed her in Keri's lap. And then in front of the entire town, he sat next to her and pulled her close.

She stiffened for a moment out of instinct then relaxed into his side, soaking up his warmth.

"This doesn't count as our date, you know," he said.

"And here I thought I could mark that off my to-do list." It felt good to tease him back, and she got the oddest sensation that Sammi was smiling down on her.

Simon lowered his mouth close to her ear. "I have something else to put on your to-do list."

Shivers that had nothing to do with the chill of the night raced over her skin. She had no idea how to respond, but she was saved by the lamplights in the park going out one by one and the Dickens carolers launching into "O Come All Ye Faithful."

All around her, people started to join in. When Simon added his deep voice to the chorus, she looked up at him in surprise. There was just enough ambient light for her to see his shadowed profile. As if he sensed her gaze, he looked down at her in a way that made all the sounds around her fade. She still thought she might wake up at some point to find the past few weeks had been a dream, some parts heartbreaking but others wonderful. Because how likely was it that fate would deal her such a blow with Sammi's and Ben's deaths followed by an awakening of her heart toward someone totally unexpected?

Simon kissed her forehead, and she closed her eyes to listen to the music. One carol led into another until the carolers began singing "Silver Bells," and tears stung her eyes.

"What's wrong?" Simon asked.

Keri hadn't realized she'd shown any outward sign of sadness. "This was Sammi's favorite Christmas carol. I can still hear her singing it." She'd had a beautiful voice, would likely have been in the school's choir if not for her basketball schedule.

"Maybe she's singing along now."

She liked the sound of that, and by suggesting it Simon had settled a little more firmly in her heart.

As the last strands of the song drifted on the air, the mayor turned the switch and the big cedar tree in the front of city hall came alive with lights. Then the cascade of snowflake lights on the utility poles up and down Main Street and the lights hanging back and forth across the street started being lit to claps and lots of oohs and ahhs. Even Hannah started to clap, eliciting laughs from Simon, Keri and several people near them.

After the lighting ceremony, the carolers sang "We Wish You a Merry Christmas" as the crowd dispersed. Simon took Hannah to allow Keri to crutch her way back to his truck. For a startled moment, she felt as though they were a family just like any other leaving the festivities.

But they weren't. Hannah wasn't their daughter, and Keri and Simon had shared nothing more than some very hot making out. Probably very much like what Simon had engaged in with any number of women. That thought soured her mood, but she didn't let it show. No good could come of letting him know his liaisons bothered her.

"You okay?" Simon asked as he pulled into her driveway a few minutes later.

"Yeah, just tired. Looking forward to getting some sleep." As they walked in the house, she didn't act as if anything out of the ordinary had happened the last time they'd been in her living room.

When Simon came out from placing a half-asleep Hannah in her crib, he moved toward Keri as if he wanted to finish what they'd started that morning. But despite how her heart beat faster the closer he came, she wasn't ready to go that far. Something she couldn't quite name stood in her way. Did she have some lingering doubt about him? Did seeing Carter again bring it out? Did part of her resent him for making her see her brother for what he really was? Before he reached her, she casually walked toward the door and opened it.

"Thank you for everything you did today. I really appreciate it."

Simon stopped in his tracks and stared at her, a touch of confusion tugging at his features. "You don't want me to stay." It wasn't a question.

"I just need some time alone." She fought the urge to try to explain more.

He nodded and walked straight for the open door. He was halfway through it when he stopped and took a step backward. He placed one hand on each side of her face and leaned down to kiss her. Long, deep, thorough. This wasn't a simple peck goodbye. It felt more like a brand on her soul.

"Sweet dreams," he whispered against her lips before disappearing into the night.

It took her several moments to regain enough strength to close and lock the door.

Sweet dreams, ha! After that kiss, she was more likely to have hot, sheet-twisting dreams. And Simon knew it.

WORK KEPT SIMON BUSY the next couple of days. It was as though everyone with any inclination to break the law felt the need to do so before the end of the year, like their New Year's resolution was going to be to give up crime for good. He crisscrossed the county dealing with everything from a domestic abuse situation that left him wondering how some people ever thought they were suitable for marriage to the theft of an ATV by a couple of teenagers who'd had a little too much to drink and thought they would make him chase them over half the damn county.

Each morning, he glanced toward the bakery but didn't darken the door. Though he'd left Keri with a kiss fresh on her lips and mind, it'd been clear she hadn't wanted him to stay the night. Whether it was because of her grief for Sammi, the tense situation with Carter or confusion about him, he was giving her time to think. Isn't that what women always needed, time to think and sort out their feelings?

Wasn't he one to talk? He'd done little other than think about her since he'd walked away with the taste of her lips still on his. Even when he was cuffing offenders or filling out the reams of paperwork every arrest came with, images of her floated in and out of his mind. Her smile, her tough-girl attitude, the feel of her skin next to his.

At the end of another crazy shift two days after he'd last seen her, he didn't feel like going home. Even tossing back a few at the Frothy Stein didn't appeal to him. It was rare that he got restless like this, but when he did only one thing ever helped. So he drove out to Vista Hills and headed for the barn.

"Hey," Nathan said as he and Ryan noticed Simon. "What's up?"

"Thought I'd go for a ride. Been a while."

"Something bothering you?" Ryan asked.

"Other than spending too much damn time in my patrol car and wanting to smack sense into stupid people, nope."

"Heard those kids gave you a good chase," Ryan said.

"Yeah, they'll be sorry when Santa brings them a date with the judge."

Simon went to the stall where Rusty, the big red horse he favored for trail rides, stood. "Hey, fella. Feel like stretching your legs?"

"How's Keri doing?" Nathan asked as Simon tossed a saddle onto Rusty's back.

He shrugged. "Okay, I guess. Haven't seen her in a couple of days."

He caught the meaningful glance between his brothers but chose to ignore it.

"Thought you two were an item now."

"Evidently not." Damn if he didn't say the words out loud, ones he hadn't realized he'd been letting fester. Is that what he wanted, to be a one-woman man? Why now? Why with Keri?

He was surprised when his brothers didn't question him further. They just let him lead Rusty out of the barn, mount up and head off to the trail that led to the highest ridgeline on the ranch. It'd be cold up there today, but he didn't care. He needed something to smack some sense into him, to clear his head of all the questions that wouldn't leave him be.

An hour later he reached a spot that looked down on the lower elevations that stretched west from Blue Falls. The wind blew from the north, bringing cooler temperatures down from the Plains. He lifted his jacket collar against it as he slid out of the saddle and tied Rusty's reins around a small oak sapling.

He walked to the edge of the ridge and stared out at a distant bank of clouds moving quickly southward. For the first time in days, he felt as if he could take a really deep breath and let distractions fall away like the land in front of him. He focused his thoughts on Keri, letting them drift wherever they wanted to go. After several minutes, he'd come to the realization that at some point things hadn't just changed between them. Something had changed inside him, a fundamental shift in who he was. He couldn't pinpoint when or precisely why, but those things didn't matter.

What did matter was that he wanted to be with her and not just for a couple of casual dates before he moved on. For the first time ever, he could only think of one woman. And the thought of her with anyone but him drove him crazy. Sometime between delivering to her the worst news of her life and holding her next to him at the Christmas lighting ceremony, he'd started falling for her. Hard.

But how did she feel? One minute, she was the old Keri who didn't want anything to do with him. The next, she was kissing him and running her hands over his back as if she was hungry and he was dinner. And the next she was somewhere in between.

He didn't want to pressure her, not when she was still getting used to her new life without her sister and raising Hannah. But he couldn't deny he wanted an answer to the question of whether she felt the way he did or if he should just move along. He hated the idea of the latter and was going to make sure she didn't pull away before he'd really shown her what she did to him.

After several more minutes of staring out toward the horizon, he pulled himself back onto Rusty's back and headed for the barn. As he listened to the clip-clop of Rusty's hooves, a plan started forming in his mind. By the time he reached the main part of the ranch, he couldn't get Rusty taken care of fast enough.

When he walked out of the barn, his brothers were nowhere to be seen. Ryan was probably back at his shop making his furniture, and he could picture Nathan at home with Grace and Evan. He was banking on the fact that Brooke would still be in the ranch kitchen, however, taking care of the guests' dinner. He stepped through the back door and found her slicing pieces of coconut cake.

Brooke looked up and smiled. "Come by for a free meal?"

He took off his hat and sauntered toward the kitchen island where she stood. "I would never say no to your cooking. After all, I do believe I was the first one to propose to you because of it."

She laughed at the memory of her first night on the ranch, before she'd officially been hired. He'd thought then maybe he'd like to go out with her, but that was before it'd become obvious that she'd had eyes for his youngest brother and the feeling was mutual.

"So sorry, I'm off the market," she said. "But I know someone who isn't."

"That's why I'm here."

Brooke looked up with wide eyes. "It is?"

"Tomorrow is Keri's birthday. I know she probably doesn't think I remember that, but it was always close to the Christmas festival so it sort of stuck in my head."

"Uh-huh."

He ignored her teasing, figuring he was due some for all he'd dished out over the years. "I want to take her out, but she'll need a babysitter. I mean, I like Hannah—"

"But she'd be the world's tiniest third wheel."

"Yeah."

"Sure, I'd love to watch her."

"Great, thanks." He hesitated for a moment, growing uncharacteristically embarrassed at the rest of his request. "Do you think you could keep her overnight?"

Brooke's smile widened. "Oh, that kind of date."

It would be if he had anything to say about it.

"I just don't want her thinking she has to hurry back."

"Sure."

"Don' tell Grace, but you're my favorite sister-in-law."

Brooke slid the last piece of cake onto a dessert plate. "Now, why do I think that story will change as soon as you need something from her?"

He lifted his hand to his heart in mock affront. "I'm wounded."

Brooke shook her head. "If Keri was anyone else, I'd feel obligated to warn her. But I think she can probably hold her own with you."

Of that he had no doubt.

"So, where are you taking her? Dinner and movie? Dancing?"

"No, but I've got the perfect idea." Simon leaned over and planted a kiss on Brooke's jaw. "Thank you."

"You're welcome."

"Hey, that's my wife you're kissing," Ryan said as he stepped in the back door.

Simon turned and headed toward the same door. "And I'm her favorite brother-in-law." He tipped Ryan's hat halfway off on his way by him.

"What's with you?" Ryan asked.

"I have a date."

"You always have a date."

But this one wasn't like any of the others. If he was being honest, this one made him nervous.

Chapter Eleven

"Where are we going?" Keri asked as Simon passed the city limits of Blue Falls heading south.

"You'll see."

"Since when are you all supersecret guy?"

"Since it's your birthday, and you should have at least one surprise on your birthday."

Keri stared across the truck at Simon. "How do you know it's my birthday? Did Sunshine tell you?"

He glanced toward her before returning his attention to the road in front of them. "I've been to a few of your birthday parties, remember?"

"That was ages ago. How could you remember what day it was? Guys don't remember that stuff."

"Now I feel offended on behalf of my gender."

She laughed and looked out the windshield just as they passed into Kendall County.

"It was always right around the Christmas festival," he finally said. "So I remembered it the other night."

The night she'd nearly pushed him out the door. The following two days had been interminably long, days in which she'd alternated between telling herself she'd done the right thing and kicking herself in the butt. It'd scared her how much she'd missed him until he'd shown up right at closing last night and told her he was taking her out and that he'd even arranged for babysitting for Hannah.

"Or maybe you've been abusing the power of your office and you ran a background check on me."

He looked at her in mock surprise. "How did you know? I should really arrest you, you know."

"For what?"

"The serial spread of cavities from all the bakery's sugary treats."

"Are you kidding? I'm keeping dentists all over the Hill Country in business. I hear they're going to give me an award."

This time, Simon was the one who laughed. "Brooke was right about you. You give as good as you get."

"You should have remembered that about me, too."

She tried three more times to get him to reveal their destination, but he wasn't budging. Eventually, she figured out it was somewhere in San Antonio. He'd told her to dress casually, so it wasn't some fancy restaurant. It wasn't until he took an exit off I-35 that she realized where they were going.

"We're going to a Spurs game?"

"Yep."

"Awesome!"

He laughed. "First time I've had that response on a date."

"Somehow I doubt that."

He gave her a funny look, and she realized how that entire exchange could be interpreted. And if their hot-and-heavy session on the couch was any indication, going even further with Simon would indeed be awesome.

When they parked and got out of the truck, Simon asked, "You okay to walk that far?"

"Yeah, the ankle's still tender, but I'm glad to finally be rid of those crutches."

"I don't know. I thought Gimpy was a cute nickname for you."

She swatted him on the shoulder, which had no effect since he was wearing a thick jacket. He reached out and took her hand in his, enveloping her in a warmth that spread out much farther than her palm as they walked in with the rest of the crowd. It might not be a candlelit dinner in a fancy restaurant, but this suddenly felt like a real date. And her heart performed a little dance of joy at that thought. She knew it was only for a few hours, but for the first time since Sammi's death she felt free. She wouldn't give up Hannah for the world, but it was nice to have an evening to relax and enjoy herself, to refuel.

Once inside, they made for the concession stand and came away with barbecue nachos, hot dogs and sodas.

"Too bad they don't have birthday cake," Simon said. "Though I'd have to grow another hand to carry it."

Keri grinned at Simon. "Are you saying I got too much food?"

"I would never comment on the amount of food a woman was eating."

"Hey, you're smarter than you look."

When they reached their seats, Keri couldn't believe it. Only a few rows back and at midcourt. "These are fantastic seats."

And she was beginning to think he really was an awesome date.

They watched the Spurs and the Grizzlies warm up on the court as they ate. She licked nacho cheese off her finger. "Ah, the best in sports arena cuisine."

Simon leaned close to her ear. "You know, I could do that for you."

Heat raced up her neck into her cheeks.

"Behave," she said quietly so the woman sitting on her other side wouldn't hear.

"What if I don't want to?"

Lord, how was she going to get through this game if he kept whispering in her ear like that?

And yet she had to admit a part of her liked it.

As the game started, she felt more and more of her worries fading into the background. She'd loved basketball from an early age, and watching professional athletes who excelled at the game live gave her a rush. She scooted to the edge of her seat as the Spurs got a breakaway.

"Come on, come on. Put it in the basket."

The point guard drove toward the basket and got fouled. Only the ref didn't call it.

"You've got to be kidding me!" she called out.

Simon chuckled behind her, drawing her attention.

"What?"

"Nothing. You're just fun to watch."

While she'd been absorbed in watching the game, he'd been watching her. Her skin tingled at that thought.

"You know how much I like basketball. What did you expect?"

"Exactly this." And he actually looked happy about that.

At the beginning of the second half, Simon bought some cotton candy. "It's not birthday cake, but it's pure sugar." He pulled a piece of the cotton candy off and placed it in front of her mouth. She accepted it then watched mesmerized as Simon licked the remains of the sticky confection off his fingers.

She'd bet a month of bakery profits that her face was every bit as pink as the cotton candy. Startled by how much she wanted him, she returned her attention to the game. Though it was an exciting second half and the Spurs eventually won the game, Simon's presence next to her made it difficult to concentrate on the action.

On their way out, Simon took her hand again as if it was the most natural action in the world. When they reached his truck, she tugged on his hand to stop him. He turned slowly and just how handsome he was hit her full force.

"Thank you for tonight," she said. "This was a great birthday present."

His mouth quirked up at the edge. "Good enough to get a kiss?"

"If it's a present, there shouldn't be any payment required."

"Does that mean you don't want to kiss me?"

Keri took a step closer and pushed up onto her toes. "I didn't say that." She slid her arms around his neck and kissed him with all the contained desire she'd been feeling all evening.

His strong arms pulled her body against his as he deepened the kiss. How had she seen Simon in town all these years and never realized he could make her feel as if she was going up in flames from the inside out?

Someone nearby whistled, making Keri realize what a display they were putting on for a good chunk of San Antonio. When she pulled away, she noticed a group of teenage boys looking in their direction and laughing as they walked toward their own vehicles.

"I think that's what they call a public display of affection," Simon said.

She smiled and slid into the truck when he opened the door for her. Normally she would have been fading toward sleep by this point, but there was no room for fatigue when her entire body was vibrating with an excitement she would have sworn was impossible a month ago. Truth be told, she didn't want this night to end. But she had to be grateful for the brief reprieve and accept that it was back to normal life as soon as his truck ate up the miles between San Antonio and Blue Falls. At least she had a little more time to hold his hand in the dark, enjoying that simple pleasure.

The drive went by too quickly. As they rolled into Blue Falls, the town was quiet except for the crowd at the Blue Falls Music Hall and several cars parked outside the Frothy Stein.

When Simon made the turn toward her house instead of heading to the ranch to pick up Hannah, she looked at him. "Is Brooke bringing Hannah to the house?"

"Nope."

"Then shouldn't we be going the other way?"

He glanced toward her. "Not tonight."

It took a moment for the appropriate cog to slide into place in her brain. When it did, the warmth that sluiced through her body put what she'd felt earlier to shame. It was as if every place he'd touched during their time on the couch a few mornings ago tingled with memories.

"Do Brooke and Ryan know they're keeping Hannah all night?"

He smiled. "Yes. And before you ask, they don't mind at all. I'm thinking Brooke might be hoping it'll put Ryan in the mood for some kidlets of their own."

It felt wrong to pawn Hannah off on someone else, especially so soon after... No, she wasn't going to think about Sammi now. Except that a sudden image of her sister giving her two thumbs-up and a wicked grin was so clear it made her wonder if Sammi had somehow put it in her brain. She smiled at the image and let her guilt go.

As Simon parked in her driveway, Keri unhooked her seat belt and slid out of the truck. It was difficult to contain a smile as she headed toward the house.

"Hey, where are you running off to so fast?" Simon asked from behind her.

"I have an entire night alone. I'm going to take advantage of it and sleep for a full eight hours."

Simon closed the distance between them and snagged her around the waist. "Who said anything about you spending the night alone?"

"You're sleepy, too?"

"Not particularly."

She couldn't contain the smile any longer. "What did you have in mind?"

He pulled her closer and lowered his mouth toward hers. "I think you know exactly what I have in mind." And then he showed her with a kiss so deep and hungry that she had to grip his arms to stay upright.

Simon kissed her all the way into the house and kicked the door closed behind him. There was no doubt how this night was going to end up, and she thought they might not even have to remove their clothes. The heat was building between them to a level where their clothing might just burn off before they got around to buttons and zippers.

As quickly as he'd pulled her into his arms, Simon pulled back and looked at her.

"What's wrong?"

He shook his head slowly back and forth. "Nothing. Are you okay with this?"

She wasn't sure if anything he could have said would have surprised her more. While she didn't think he'd ever force any woman into anything she didn't want to do, wouldn't have to, something about the look in his eyes and the…concern in his voice touched a spot deep inside her.

"I'm sure."

He hesitated a moment more before kissing her again, this time with a tenderness that made her fall a little in love with him.

Then, as he had the night she'd fallen off the ladder, he scooped her into his arms and carried her slowly toward her bedroom before setting her on her feet again in the dim light. But unlike their frenzied couch aerobics, this time they moved slowly. Each time she unclasped one of his shirt buttons or he removed another piece of her clothing, they stopped to kiss and run their fingertips over each other's skin.

By the time she stood in nothing but her underwear, she was throbbing with need.

Simon ran his hand through her hair to the nape of her neck. "You're beautiful."

Happiness spread within her like the opening of a flower. "You're not so bad yourself."

He lifted her again, but this time he didn't put her down until she was stretched out on her bed. He held her gaze as he removed first her bra and then her panties. She should have been embarrassed, but she wasn't. As he stood to his full height and shucked his jeans and briefs, she still didn't look away. Her heart thudded hard against her rib cage.

He was beautiful, too. All lanky, sinewy muscle perfectly made for what they were about to do.

A flutter of nervousness made itself known as he slid into bed beside her and pulled her comforter over them both. He caressed her cheek.

"If you want to stop at any point, just tell me." He

smiled a little. "It might be the hardest thing I've ever done, but I'll stop."

She looked deep into his eyes and felt the absolute truth of what she was about to say. "I don't want to stop."

His hand came to rest on her hip, then slowly moved up her ribs, teasing at her breast just enough to drive her half-crazy. His lips followed the trail his hand blazed, and when his mouth reached her breast his tongue caused her to arch against him. That movement evidently stoked a flame within him because he shifted over her and used his knee to spread her legs. She felt as if her heartbeat was pulsing in every single inch of her body.

When Simon reached down between them, Keri threw her head back and gave in to pure sensation. Tingles and vibrations and spasms. And the very real possibility she might scream if he didn't finish what he'd started. His mouth captured hers at the same moment he slid into her, so her cry of pleasure was lost somewhere inside of him.

Simon stilled his body for a few moments, his only movements those of his mouth as his tongue danced with hers. Then he eased himself almost out before pushing back in with the same maddening slowness. Her body was screaming for a faster pace, animalistic in its need. So she moved against him, letting him know without words exactly what she wanted.

He responded with a growl that turned on yet another area of desire within her.

"You're driving me crazy," he said next to her ear.

"Then I suggest you do something about that."

He did, quickening the pace with each stroke until they both were panting. Keri wrapped her legs around his hips at the same moment he wrapped his arms around her back, pulling her even closer to his thrusts. She threw out her arms and gripped the pillows as if they were going to keep her from bucking right off the bed into the air.

All of her focus zeroed in on the feel of Simon and the pinnacle she was climbing frantically toward. It came only moments after Simon stiffened all over and found his release. He collapsed into a heap of exhausted flesh and bone next to her. Keri didn't move, wasn't sure she could even if she tried. If she'd ever wondered what a bowl of cooked spaghetti noodles felt like, now she knew.

"I'm going to have to resign from my job," Simon said, prompting her to turn her head toward him.

"What? Why?"

"Because I'm pretty sure I just shot any ability to walk or think coherently."

She smiled. "So, you're saying I could do anything to you right now and you wouldn't be able to put up a fight?"

He found the energy to lift an eyebrow. "What did you have in mind?"

She rolled on top of him, loving the feel of power that welled within her. With her gaze locked on his, she lowered her mouth to his chest and started kissing all that warm, salty flesh.

"I think it's time to reciprocate." She flicked her tongue across one of his nipples, eliciting a strangled groan from him. Other parts of him woke up and took notice, as well.

"You're trying to do me in for good," he said.

"Don't tell me the famous playboy Simon Teague can't stand a bit of teasing himself."

He moved so quickly, rolling her onto her back, that she gasped then laughed. But she stopped laughing when she saw the serious look on his face.

"You're not like anyone else, Keri."

What did he mean by that?

"And I want you to know that half the things that are

said about me aren't true. Just because I go out and have a good time doesn't mean I've slept with half the women in town. Not even close." He planted a soft kiss on her lips. "And not in a long time."

His words were doing funny things to her heart, things that were going to make her more vulnerable than she ever wanted to be. But she was powerless to fight it as he made love to her again, this time slowly and with lots of kissing and gentle exploration. As she drifted toward sleep sometime in the wee hours, her heart acknowledged the truth.

She was falling in love with Simon Teague.

SIMON FELT LIKE ONE OF the addicts he'd had to arrest throughout his law enforcement career. But his drug of choice was a beautiful, strong woman named Keri Mehler. When he wasn't at work, he was helping her at the bakery, stealing kisses in her office, or swirling her around the dance floor at the music hall. She didn't even have to ask for a babysitter. He knew exactly how his family felt about his relationship with Keri by the steady stream of Teagues lined up to babysit Hannah.

"Why do I think I'm going to turn around one day and she's going to be in baby cowgirl boots and astride a horse?' Keri asked as she watched Nathan walk off with her niece after a Sunday lunch with his family.

"Would that be so bad?"

"No, I guess not. Though she's going to be a basketball player too."

Simon pulled her inside the dim interior of the barn and into his arms. "What if she wants to be a ballerina?"

"That's okay, too, though she'll be out of luck getting advice from me."

"Oh, I don't know. You have some pretty good moves."

Ones that were leading to a distinct lack of sleep for him the past few days.

Keri glanced outside as if embarrassed that someone might overhear their conversation.

"No use worrying now. Pretty sure they know what we've been up to."

She dropped her forehead against his chest, causing him to laugh.

"Come on, let's go for a ride."

A few minutes later, she was seated in front of him as they meandered up one of the trails. When they reached a meadow where his mom liked to come to paint, he pulled Rusty to a stop and dismounted. Then he reached up and helped Keri down. As he tied Rusty's reins to a tree branch, Keri walked a few steps away and looked down the slope.

"It's pretty here," she said.

"You should see it in the spring. It's covered up with wildflowers, especially bluebonnets."

She grew quiet, and he possessed enough instinct to know that something was on her mind.

"Something bothering you?" he asked as he wrapped his arms around her from behind.

She didn't answer at first, and a nugget of worry settled inside him.

"I've been having a really nice time with you lately," she said.

"The feeling's mutual." He kissed her temple to illustrate that fact.

She grew quiet again, as if she were struggling with whether to give voice to whatever was plaguing her thoughts.

"Whatever it is, might be best to just say it." Though

part of him was screaming at him to stop inviting potential bad news.

"Why did you become a cop when everyone else in your family works at the ranch?"

"I couldn't resist the stylish uniform and road to riches."

She stepped out of his arms, took a couple of steps away then turned toward him. That's when he knew she wasn't in the mood for his teasing.

"The truth, Simon. Please."

He should have known things couldn't go on the way they had been, that at some point the curves in the road were going to lead back to Carter.

"It sounds corny."

She didn't respond, just kept staring at him with her eyes demanding answers.

He shoved his hands into the pockets of his coat. "Because I had the crazy thought that maybe I could help keep kids from making stupid mistakes like Carter and I did."

Her eyes widened as if she hadn't expected that answer, and he wondered what she could have thought he'd say. Contrary to his teasing, it wasn't the profusion of polyester and less-than-stellar paychecks.

She turned and took a few steps away from him to stare out across the meadow. "I can't stop thinking about him. Despite everything he's done, I've missed him. Besides Hannah, he's all the family I have left. I keep thinking that something could happen to him, and I'd feel horrible for not helping him when I had the chance."

"You have helped him, Keri, many times. He might not realize it, but you're helping him now."

She angled herself back toward him. "Then why doesn't it feel like it?"

"Because the right thing isn't always the easiest."

She looked so heartbroken that he searched for anything that might make her feel better.

"But," he said, "maybe you can reconnect with him without letting him take advantage of you."

"I haven't had a very good history with that." She sighed deeply. "But I'll think about it."

For Keri's sake, he hoped she and her brother could repair their relationship. But if Carter hurt her again, he was going to live to regret it.

Chapter Twelve

Keri sat in the room that had once been Carter's and asked herself for the umpteenth time if she'd made a dreadful mistake by not letting Carter stay here, by not giving him a job. Part of her knew she'd done the right thing, however painful, but another asked what kind of sense it made to push away what little family she had left.

There had to be some sort of middle ground.

Determined to find it, she left the room and went to bundle Hannah in her little coat for an unexpected outing.

"We have to be strong, Hannah," she said as she zipped up the miniature coat and pulled up the hood. "Your uncle Carter has to learn some tough lessons, but we want him to know we love him, anyway."

Hannah responded with a slobbery grin and some waving of her little hands. Keri picked her up and hugged her close, wishing with all her heart she could give Hannah her mother and father back.

Once they were in the car and Keri got the heat going she drove through Blue Falls, making circuits of the parking lots at all the hotels and B and B inns. By the time she'd finished circling the lot at the last one, she realized Carter might not have been exaggerating when he'd said he would have to sleep in his car. Granted, Texas wasn't the coldest place in the country, but it was still too cold to sleep in a car.

Starting to feel desperate to find him, she drove up and down each street, searching for the little blue Honda he'd been driving since high school. Somehow in all his wanderings, he'd managed to keep it running. She was on the verge of calling Simon for some help when she finally spotted the car in the darkest end of the parking lot next to the lake.

Her heart broke that her brother had been reduced to homelessness.

She parked with her headlights shining on his car. He either hadn't been asleep or the sound of her car woke him, but he sat up shading his eyes from the light.

"Oh, Carter," she said, then got out of the car.

He didn't open his window until she got close.

"What are you doing here?" he asked, distance in his tired voice.

"I want to talk."

"You've already made your feelings clear."

"Don't make me the bad guy here, Carter." She adopted the big sister tone she'd used with him when they were younger and she'd had more sway over him. "Come on back to the house."

He didn't say anything, but the flash of hope in his eyes broke her heart a little more. How had he gotten himself to this point in his life?

When they returned to the house, Keri placed Hannah in the playpen in the living room and headed to the kitchen to make coffee. While it was brewing, she sliced off two thick pieces of lemon cake. She listened as Carter came in the front door and started talking to Hannah.

Keri poured two cups of coffee and placed them and the slices of cake and forks on a tray. With a deep breath to fortify herself, she walked into the living room. Carter sat on the edge of the coffee table and leaned on the side of the playpen. When he noticed her, he tried to hide the fact he had to wipe his eyes.

"She's gotten so big," he said.

"Babies grow fast."

He reached into the playpen, hesitated a moment, then rubbed his hand over Hannah's baby-fine hair. "I still can't believe Sammi's gone."

Keri swallowed against the sudden lump in her throat and blinked several times to fight back her own tears. She placed the tray on the table and sank onto the couch. Slowly, Carter moved from his perch on the table to the opposite end of the couch. For a few minutes, neither of them said anything as they ate their cake and warmed themselves with the fresh coffee.

"The cake's delicious as usual," Carter finally said.

Keri sat down her cup and empty plate. "Where have you been, Carter?"

He shrugged. "Different places, most recently Texas City."

She sighed. "I really needed you when Sammi died."

"I know. I'm so sorry." His words rang with truth, and hope bloomed inside her that maybe he really had changed. Or at least was trying.

"What are your plans? Are you staying around this time?"

He rubbed his palms up his thighs toward his knees. "I want to. I…just have some things I have to take care of first."

She looked him full in the face. "Are you in some kind of trouble? Because if you are, I won't have it brought into my home. I won't put Hannah in danger."

"No."

He seemed to be telling the truth, but she got the distinct feeling he was hiding something. Maybe if they took baby steps, he'd eventually feel comfortable enough to tell her. Small steps were all she felt equipped to take right now, anyway.

"You can stay in your old room," she said.

"Does this mean I can work at the bakery, too?"

"No. I can't afford another employee right now. You'll have to find a job on your own."

He looked about to protest, but then he clamped his mouth shut and nodded. "Thank you for letting me stay."

"I don't begin to claim I understand you or your choices, but you're still my brother and I love you. I can't leave you out there to freeze in your car. But if you've lied to me or you put Hannah in one ounce of danger, you're out of here and you won't ever be welcome back."

"I understand."

Though it had been a short conversation, Keri was a lot more tired than she'd been only a few minutes before. "It's time Hannah went to bed, and I need to go to sleep, too."

"Okay."

As she stood, Carter jumped to his feet and scooped Hannah out of the playpen into his arms. "It's bedtime for you, sweetie pie," he said.

Keri couldn't help smiling at the image they made and hoped that there were many more where that one came from. Without Ben, Hannah could really use an uncle in her life. As long as that uncle was responsible and stuck around instead of disappearing and breaking her heart.

OVER THE NEXT FEW DAYS, Keri stayed busy at the bakery, so busy that she barely saw Carter. He was beating every available bush looking for a job, but so far no one had hired him. She was afraid that the "everyone knows everything about everyone" aspect of Blue Falls was working against him. After all, who would want to hire someone who had an arrest record and might skip town at any moment? She considered changing her mind about having him work at the bakery, but she held her ground. He had to make his own way. It was enough that she was housing and feeding him.

But it was hard to ignore the increasingly desperate look on his face when she did see him. The feeling that he was hiding something increased, but she was honestly too afraid to ask what it might be. They were slowly rebuilding their relationship, and she feared the truth might shatter that tentative progress.

After another long day at the bakery, she should be sleeping but couldn't turn off her whirling thoughts. Instead, she lay on the couch and watched the clock slowly tick away the minutes. It was after eleven, and Carter still hadn't come home. She reminded herself that he'd said he was meeting up with an old friend tonight and that he wouldn't be home until late. That he hadn't fled town again, leaving her to hold together their family and its legacy.

Knocking on the front door surprised her. Maybe Carter had forgotten his key.

When she reached the front door and opened it, however, it wasn't her brother on the porch. Simon stood there holding the biggest bouquet of flowers she'd ever seen, a rainbow of colors and types.

"What in the world?" she asked as her heart did a tap dance in her chest.

"Brenna McLaren owed me a favor."

"She opened the flower shop at this hour?"

"I might have appealed to her romantic side."

Her heart nearly staggered to a halt until she realized it wasn't Brenna he was interested in, not with the way he was looking at Keri over the top of that bouquet.

"We've both been working too much," he said. "I've missed you." And with those three words, she completely fell head over heels for him.

"I've missed you, too," she whispered.

She stepped back and he walked inside. He scanned the room. "Carter here?"

"No."

"Good." He deposited the flowers onto her coffee table, then pulled her into his arms.

"Why haven't I seen you?" she asked as she looked up at his handsome face.

"I heard Carter is staying with you, and I figured you needed time to be with him. But I don't want him to come between us again," he said.

"He won't."

She pushed thoughts of her brother and his problems aside because she wanted nothing more in that moment than to be with Simon. She hadn't realized just how much she'd missed him until she'd opened the door and seen him standing there. She took his hand and led him into her bedroom. A glance into the crib revealed that Hannah was still fast asleep, her little arm around the bunny that had become her favorite companion.

Simon stepped up behind Keri and wrapped his arms around her waist. "If you let me keep coming over, you might need to think about a nursery."

"Why? She's too young to really know anything."

"But you want her to sleep, and I'm not always going to want to be quiet," he said next to her ear.

Her entire body flushed with a heat that had her dragging him to the bed. "Until then, let's see if you can get the job done and still be quiet."

He gave her a wicked grin. "That sounds like a challenge."

"Take it any way you like it."

As it turned out, it wasn't Simon who had the most trouble keeping quiet while they made love. It was her, and with good reason. When he held her close afterward, she realized she couldn't give him up. She never wanted to see him with another woman because… She hesitated at the full impact of the truth but accepted it just as she was falling asleep. She was in love with Simon Teague. Totally, irrevocably, crazy in love.

SIMON WAS GLAD HE'D SUGGESTED that Keri make peace with Carter. Since she'd invited him back into his childhood home, he'd noticed a lessening of the sorrow that seemed to be her constant companion even when she'd seemed happy on the outside.

She'd even decided to start on converting the bedroom that had been Sammi's and hers into a room for Hannah, one that could start as a nursery and change as she grew. That's why he was currently packing a ton of paint and related supplies into her house. When he reached the bedroom, she was sitting on one of the twin beds looking at a photo album. He placed the supplies on the plastic-covered floor and went to sit by her.

Smiling pictures of the three Mehler siblings stared up at them.

"I remember this day like it was yesterday," she said as she pointed to a photo of the three of them soaking wet at Sea World. "We sat in the front row during the whale show." She ran her fingertips over those younger versions of her and her siblings.

"You sure you're ready to do this?" he asked.

She slowly closed the album and looked around the room. "Yeah. This room should be Hannah's just like it was her mother's."

"And her aunt's."

She shrugged as if that part didn't matter.

Before he could stand and get started moving the last of the furniture out of the room so they could paint, his two-way radio squawked at him.

"Sorry. I'm on call tonight. Pete's sick as a dog."

"It's okay."

He left the room and answered. "Yeah?"

"We've gotten a call about a break-in at the Yost residence out on Trailblazer Road."

Damn, that was the fourth such call in a week. Somebody evidently pulling a Christmas-shopping-by-theft scheme. "Okay, I'm on my way."

When he clipped the radio back onto his belt, he noticed Keri standing at the doorway to the bedroom.

"You've got to go?"

"Yeah, I'm sorry."

"No need to apologize. It's part of who you are."

He wondered if she was okay with that, or if she was having second thoughts, wanting someone who wouldn't be rushing out after bad guys at odd hours.

"If Carter gets back in time, I'll just put him to work," she said.

Simon crossed to her in a few long strides and pulled her into his arms. He wanted to tell her how he felt about her, but words failed him. So he kissed her with a mixture of passion and tenderness that he hoped did the talking for him. What told him more than anything how much he wanted to be with her was his reluctance to go searching for some thief. He wanted to stay here helping her paint, stealing kisses and wrapping up the night by making love to her.

Instead, he ended the kiss and grabbed his hat on the way to the door.

Two hours later, he'd taken statements from the theft victims and was on the way back to the office to compare notes with those for the other thefts when he noticed a light moving around in Bruno Derring's house. A light that shouldn't be there since Bruno was out of town visiting his daughter and grandkids in California.

Simon pulled off to the side of the road and cut both the lights and engine on the SUV. He unclipped the holster on his sidearm and slipped quietly from the vehicle. The chill of the night stung his cheeks as he eased along the darker side of the driveway. He stopped and faded into the shadows when he heard a door close around back. As he waited for the perp to appear, he eased his gun out of the holster and fixed his grip on it.

But when the faint light of the moon illuminated the thief, his grip slipped. Hurrying back toward the road with a bag of loot was none other than Carter Mehler.

With a heavy heart, Simon stepped out of the shadows and took aim just in case he didn't know Carter like he thought he did.

"Hello, Carter."

Carter froze in his tracks, then slowly set the bag down on the ground. He showed no signs of running. Neither of those things surprised Simon. What did was when Carter looked up and revealed something totally unexpected in his eyes.

Tears.

"LET'S TRY THIS AGAIN," Simon said as he sat across the interrogation table from Carter. "Last trace I could find of you was two months ago when you were working at one of the oil refineries in Texas City. Then poof, nothing until you show up in Blue Falls again. You been stealing your way back here?"

"No."

"And why would I believe that?"

Carter looked up. "If you had no intention of believing me, why did you ask?"

"I'm hoping to get some truth out of you."

Carter lowered his gaze to his hands cuffed together atop the table. "I want to talk to Keri."

"No."

Carter's eyes met Simon's again. "What do you mean, no? I get a call."

"Then I'd suggest you call an attorney and not bother your sister with this."

"You think she's not going to hear about me in here? Pretty sure Blue Falls hasn't grown so much that the gossip doesn't fly across town in the blink of an eye."

Simon let out a long breath, remembering what he'd told Keri about wishing he could go back in time and try harder to help Carter. Maybe they wouldn't be sitting across the table as adversaries now.

"If you have any heart at all, you'll leave your sister out of this and let her live her life free of any more heartache."

Carter stared at him as if he was trying to decipher a complex code. "When did you two start talking again?"

"Stop avoiding the questions."

"Pot, meet kettle."

Simon stared at his former friend for several long moments, trying to decide what tactic to take with him. Finally, he decided a little truth on his side might elicit a similar response from Carter.

"I've been helping Keri out since Sammi's death."

Carter winced and lowered his gaze again. He might have made a lot of stupid moves in his life, but Carter was undoubtedly grieving over his oldest sister.

"I'm sorry I wasn't here," Carter said, the anger and confrontation draining out of his voice. "Thank you for doing what I should have."

Those words sounded heartfelt, and for some reason that surprised Simon.

Voices filtered in from the reception area of the station. At first, Simon shut them out to focus on the task at hand. But then he identified Keri's voice and closed his eyes, wishing she'd stayed away.

Carter must have heard his sister, too, because he shifted his attention toward the door. "Please, Simon. If you ever considered us friends, please let me talk to her."

There was a desperation to Carter's plea, something more than worry about his sister being upset at him.

"What's going on, Carter?"

"I just want to talk to my sister."

Simon had interrogated enough people to know when one wasn't going to talk without some further impetus. Maybe Keri could provide that, though he hated the idea of her seeing her brother locked up.

"Well, that's up to her," he said. "But I wouldn't hold my breath if I were you."

When he stepped out of the interrogation room, Keri's gaze landed on him. "What's going on, Simon?"

He noticed the long-sleeved T-shirt she was wearing was splattered with the yellow paint she'd picked out for Hannah's room. He took a deep breath. No use beating around the bush.

"I arrested Carter for four counts of breaking and entering and theft."

Her mouth dropped open a little before she pressed her lips together and paced across the room. Jack, who'd been holding down the fort tonight, got up from his desk and made himself scarce.

Keri shook her head. "It's got to be a mistake."

"It's no mistake. I caught him in the act."

She looked as though she wanted to argue, to believe her brother hadn't duped her again, before her face dropped to her hands. "Why can't he get his life together?"

He didn't answer. He didn't have one.

"He wants to talk to you."

She slowly turned toward him. "You can tell him that I'll talk to him when he grows up."

He wanted so much to hold her and soothe this new hurt, but he held his ground. That look in her eyes and the stiffness of her body told him now wasn't the right time.

After she left, he stood in the same spot for a couple of minutes before retracing his steps back to Carter. When he entered the room, Carter looked up with such hope in his eyes that it felt like a physical blow.

"She doesn't want to talk to you," Simon said as he reclaimed his seat.

"I have to talk to her."

"I can't exactly make her do what she doesn't want to."

Carter propped his elbows on the table and dropped his forehead into his palms. He looked utterly broken, and suddenly Simon was a teenager again staring at his best friend with a spray paint can in his hand.

Simon leaned forward and propped his forearms on the table. "We were once friends, so I can tell there's something you're not telling me. Let me help you, man."

Carter looked up and the expression on his face was

raw and full of pain. "If you want to help me, please get Keri to talk to me."

Though he'd revealed nothing, Simon knew without a doubt there was more honesty in that plea than anything he'd heard Carter utter in years.

Chapter Thirteen

Keri cursed as she dumped an entire tray of burned muffins in the trash. Her concentration had fractured into innumerable pieces the moment she'd heard that Carter had been arrested. In a blink, she'd been zapped back to that day of his first arrest. And again, Simon was right there in the middle of it.

She knew he was only doing his job and that if Carter was guilty he deserved to be arrested, but it didn't make the situation hurt any less.

She jumped when someone tapped on the front door. Unable to sleep and with Hannah at Sunshine's house, Keri had come into the bakery early. The sky was still dark, but the streetlights illuminated Simon.

With legs that felt as if they'd been coated in lead, she trudged toward the door. When she opened it, they stood staring at each other for several seconds before he slipped inside and took her into his arms. She'd held the tears in all night, but now they fell without ceasing.

"I just can't take any more," she said next to his chest.

Simon ran his hand over her hair and made soothing sounds. "We'll get through this. You're strong, and I'm not going anywhere."

Despite her layers of sorrow, a spark lit in her heart. She liked it when he said "we" and promised to always be there. She wanted so desperately to believe it was true, but every time she started to believe the worst was over something else beat her back down. She hated feeling sorry for herself, but sometimes the feeling won over her determination to fight it.

"What am I going to do?" she asked.

He didn't answer at first, as if he were struggling with what to say. "Go talk to your brother."

She pulled back. "What?"

He framed her face with his hands. "I don't know what's going on with him, but he keeps begging me to see you."

"He probably wants bail money."

Simon shook his head. "Maybe, but maybe not. Call it gut instinct, but there's something different about him."

She pulled out of his embrace and took a few steps away. "How can you say that? You just arrested him. How is that different?"

"Keri, do you trust me?"

She met his eyes and felt the power of them, of him. "Yes."

"Then go talk to him. Something is going on, and I'm hoping he'll tell you."

"I've asked, several times. And he hasn't told me, either."

"He wasn't in jail then. He had one phone call, and he didn't call a bail bondsman or an attorney or even you. It was a number to a pay phone outside a motel in San Antonio. My instinct is telling me we really need to know who he called."

Before she realized what she was doing, she found herself nodding.

A few minutes later, she stood outside the door that led back to the Sheriff Department's five holding cells.

Simon gripped her shoulders and planted a kiss on top of her head.

"You can do this," he said.

She nodded then walked through the door.

Carter was the only occupant in the lockup, and he didn't look up at first. Only when the door shut behind her did he glance her direction then jump to his feet and come to stand next to the exterior bars.

"You came."

"What do you want, Carter?"

He looked so sad for a moment that she nearly went to him and pulled him into her arms as best she could through the iron bars.

"I need your help."

"If this is about bail, you can just forget it."

"Please, Keri. It's not for me. But I need to help someone else."

She walked a few steps closer. "What are you talking about?"

Carter gripped a bar in each hand and leaned his head against them. "A friend of mine needs help, and she's running out of time."

She noted the increasingly familiar desperation in his voice. "What do you mean? Who is this friend?"

"Someone I met when I was living in Texas City. A waitress at this diner I used to eat at." He glanced at the door to the offices outside as if he was afraid Simon might hear. "You can't tell Simon any of this."

"You're not in a position to tell me what to do."

He met her eyes, and she saw fear in his. "They'll kill her family."

Keri reached out and gripped one of the cell bars. Their conversation just got a lot more serious. "I think you better start at the beginning."

He moved closer to her. "Have you ever been in love, Keri?"

Before she thought, she glanced toward the door.

"So that's how it is," Carter said. He hesitated for a moment. "I'm happy for you, both of you. But maybe you'll understand why I did what I did."

"Please tell me you're talking about the thefts and nothing more serious."

"Her name is Josephina," he said, ignoring Keri's request. "She's the most beautiful, sweetest, kindest person you'd ever meet. So I was surprised when she seemed interested in me." Carter got a dreamy look that Keri recognized. It was how she felt when she thought of Simon. "We started dating, fell in love. I was on the verge of asking her to marry me when she got word from a man that he had her family, demanding money for their safe passage from Mexico into the U.S."

Keri gasped. "They were kidnapped?"

"Not exactly. The guy…he's a coyote. They went to him to get out of the country."

"God, Carter, you're trying to help illegal immigrants? Are you trying to get yourself killed?"

She started to step away, but he grabbed her hand.

"Her mother and sisters witnessed the murder of an American, a college kid. The man they went to demanded more money than they had. He said that either they got the full amount from Josephina or he would take them back to Mexico and turn them over to the cartel responsible for the killing."

This story just got worse and worse.

"How much does this man want?"

He quoted a figure that made her heart sink. "I have some money saved, but I lost my job when I missed too much work trying to help Josephina."

"That's why you came to me?" And she'd refused him, which no doubt led to everyone else in town doing the same. He'd turned to theft as a last alternative.

"I ran out of options, Keri. I can't let her family die. It'll kill her."

"Are you sure she's telling the truth? She's not just playing you?"

"I've never been more positive of anything in my life." He blinked back tears. "For the first time in my life, I felt like I had a purpose and direction. I wanted to be the best man I could be for her. I want to be her hero, Keri. I've never wanted anything like that before. I'd give up everything for her."

"Let me get Simon. We can work something—"

"No! The man said no cops. If he gets even a whiff of a cop, he said the deal is off."

"What am I supposed to do, then?"

"I just need a little more money. Josephina has the rest, what she and I have scraped together. We were supposed to meet the guy tonight for the exchange."

A very bad feeling curled in Keri's stomach. "So you want me to post bail so you can help smuggle illegal immigrants. How much jail time do you think you'll get for that?"

"I don't care as long as I can get them all to safety, get Josephina back with her family."

Keri stared at her brother and realized suddenly that he had grown up despite his current position. "Why didn't you just tell me this before?"

"I didn't want you to get involved. I wouldn't be asking for your help now if I had any other choice."

Keri paced the length of the holding area and back. "When are you supposed to meet this guy?"

"Eight o'clock at an old garage south of San Antonio. But I've got to meet Josephina before that."

"Where?"

Carter's eyes filled with suspicion.

"Listen, I'm not letting you run off and do this without knowing where you are," she said.

She neglected to tell him she wasn't about to let him go at all. She couldn't knowingly send the only sibling she had left into a life-threatening situation.

He gave her the meet-up location, a little motel on the south side of San Antonio.

"Okay, I'll get you out of here under one condition."

"Anything."

"You tell Simon everything you just told me."

Carter ran his hand back through his hair. "Didn't you hear the part about no cops?"

"They're more equipped to deal with this than you are. This isn't the first time this type of thing has happened. I heard a story about it on the news the other day."

Carter paced to the back of his cell and back. "I guess I don't have any choice, do I?"

"Sure you do. You can stay in that cell or you get out and let the cops do their jobs."

"Fine."

"Okay, let me go get the ball rolling." But when she stepped out into the main part of the department, Simon wasn't there. Instead, she made eye contact with Deputy Pete Kayne.

"Hey, Pete. I was looking for Simon."

"He had to run down to the courthouse, said to tell you he'd be back in a few minutes."

"Oh, okay." She glanced back toward the door that led to the holding area. Might as well go ahead and get the paperwork out of the way. She returned her attention to Pete. "I want to post bail for Carter."

Surprise registered in his expression, and she realized he must have been in the building when she'd been there the first time, when she'd said in no uncertain terms that she wasn't about to bail out her thieving brother. But she didn't offer an explanation. That she'd only give to Simon in hopes that he could somehow manage to help Carter's girlfriend and her family without putting anyone in danger. If Josephina was telling the truth, Keri didn't want to do anything that would cause her to have to go through the type of pain and loss Keri had experienced.

Being a small department, it didn't take long for Pete to do what was necessary to free Carter. She forked over the bond money, and a couple of minutes later Carter was strolling out of the cell block. Pete handed Carter back his personal effects. Carter slipped his wallet into his pocket and palmed some change.

"I'm dying for a soda. Want one?" he asked.

"No, I'm good."

She watched as he walked down the hallway that led to the restrooms and the vending area. As he passed the men's room, he must have decided he needed to make a pit stop because he pulled open the door and disappeared inside.

A few seconds later, Simon stepped in the front door. "You okay?" he asked when he saw her.

She nodded. "I need to talk to you."

He nodded toward his office. "Let's go in here."

She followed. Once inside, she sat in a chair that afforded her a view down the hallway.

"What's going on?" he asked as he propped himself against the edge of his desk.

"I found out what's been bothering Carter."

"Do I want to know?"

"Probably not." She proceeded to tell him everything Carter had shared with her.

"I swear, your brother is like a trouble magnet," he said when she finished.

Though there was a good bit of truth in his words, it still bothered her to hear them. "Be that as it may, what are we going to do? People's lives are at stake here."

"What can I do? I have to call the feds."

She'd known that would be the outcome. She just hoped Carter forgave her.

Simon heaved a sigh as he pushed away from the desk. "Let me go talk to him."

"He's in the restroom." In fact, he'd been in there a good long time.

"What?"

"I bailed him out."

Simon cursed and stalked past her and down the hallway. When he reached the restroom, he jerked the door open and stepped inside. In a blink, he was back in the hallway. "He's gone. Went out the window."

Keri raced to the exterior door and ran outside, her heart in her throat. Simon followed her. She halted suddenly when she realized the spot where she'd parked was now filled with another vehicle.

"He took my car." She spun toward Simon. "He's gone after her. Oh, my God, what have I done? He's going to get himself killed!"

Simon gripped her shoulders until she looked up at him. "We'll get him back, I promise."

"Please. I can't lose him, too."

"You won't." He steered her back toward the building and in out of the December chill. "Pete, report Keri's car as stolen, and contact immigration and the Department of Public Safety. Give them the information on that hotel that Carter called. But tell them I'm on my way."

Pete nodded and picked up the phone.

Simon grabbed his jacket from the rack where he'd hung it up only a few minutes earlier. When Keri tried to follow him, he held out his hand to stop her.

"You need to stay here, Keri."

"But he's my brother."

"And I'm going to get him. But you have to stay here where you're safe, so I don't worry about you. Here with Hannah." He said the last slowly and with deeper meaning.

Keri swallowed hard and fought tears, trying not to think about the fact that there might be shooting involved, that she would be in danger of leaving Hannah even more of an orphan if she put herself in the cross fire.

"Please bring him back safely."

Simon pulled her to him and kissed her forehead. And then he headed out the door without a word. She tried not to think about what that meant as she watched him turn on his flashers and race toward the southern edge of town.

SIMON PUSHED HIS DEPARTMENT'S SUV to its limit on the way to San Antonio. By the time he hit the city, he'd been informed that Keri's car still hadn't been located, that there was no sign of it or Carter at the motel. And no one named Josephina. Thinking she might be hiding out nearby, he didn't disagree when the other officers decided to leave the motel. Better if he approached her alone.

He parked a couple of streets over from the motel where Carter had said Josephina was waiting. It didn't take long to spot her. The lovely Hispanic woman was sitting on an old bench under a sprawling live oak tree on the opposite side of the parking lot. He might not have noticed her except for the fact she was sitting beneath a security light. He approached slowly so he wouldn't spook the other woman.

"Josephina?"

Carter's girlfriend's eyes widened in fear, and she looked as if she might bolt.

Simon held a hand palm out toward Josephina. "It's okay. I'm a friend of Carter's. My name is Simon Teague. I'm the sheriff of the county where Carter grew up."

"Simon? You used to be friends, when you were boys?"

Carter had mentioned him? He didn't think he wanted to know what his former best friend had said.

Josephina fidgeted as she looked past him. "Where's Carter?"

"I thought he was supposed to meet you here."

"He was."

"But you haven't seen him?"

She shook her head.

A very bad feeling that Carter was doing something stupid at that very moment curled in Simon's gut.

"Do you know where the meeting place with the coyote is?"

Josephina jerked in surprise. "How...how do you know about that?"

"Carter told his sister, Keri, and she told me. And unless you want something very bad to happen to Carter, you need to tell me where he's going right now."

Josephina just stared at him for a long moment before deciding she had no other choice. "I'll show you. I have to be there or the man will kill my family."

Simon didn't like taking this woman into the potential line of fire, but he wasn't left with a lot of options.

Once they were in the car, he hesitated putting the keys in the ignition. "I need to know this whole thing is on the up-and-up, that you're not just playing Carter. That I'm not driving into a trap."

Josephina clasped her hands together in her lap. "If it is a trap, it is not of my making. Carter told you what danger my family is in?"

"Yes."

"Then please know that this is the only way. If there were some other way, a legal way, I would do it in a heartbeat. I don't want my family to have to hide, to live in fear of deportation or worse. But I don't want them to be slaughtered, either. And if they go back to Mexico, that is what will happen."

There was such pain and honesty in Josephina's words that whatever doubt Simon had felt disappeared. "We'll get your family away from this guy, then deal with the consequences, okay?"

Josephina nodded. "I thank you from the bottom of my heart."

"But you have to do exactly as I say, no questions."

"Okay."

Josephina directed him to take a series of turns back to the interstate. As they headed south, civilization started to fade away. After half an hour, Josephina shifted in her seat.

"The exit is coming up on the right. There's an abandoned gas station there where we're supposed to meet the man."

Simon turned off his headlights and made a call for backup, telling them to come in quiet and dark so they didn't spook the coyote. He pulled to the side of the access road and cut the engine a good distance from the old station.

"I'm going the rest of the way on foot," he said. "You

need to stay here. Keep the doors locked and if anyone drives by, you get down."

"The man is expecting me."

Simon checked his sidearm. "You need to trust me, Josephina. Stay here."

His gut was telling him Carter was already in the midst of this potentially nasty meeting. He didn't need another civilian there, too.

Fear came off Josephina in waves, but she didn't make any move to disobey him. He slipped out of the SUV and eased the door closed. He kept to the shadows and the grassy area adjacent to the road so his boots didn't alert anyone to his approach. He probably should have waited for backup, but he didn't trust that they wouldn't blow everything, putting Carter and Josephina's family in more danger than they were already in.

Simon slowed when he got close to the abandoned lot and circled around the outskirts to the darker area next to the building. Though the station obviously hadn't been operational for years, a security light still sat at the edge of the lot and shed faint illumination on the two men facing each other.

Carter, the damn fool, faced a dark-haired guy who looked as if he could break the backs of professional wrestlers.

"Where is the woman?" the guy asked.

"It doesn't matter," Carter said. "I have the money you wanted."

"Toss it to me," he said.

"I want to see Josephina's family first."

The guy hesitated before taking a few steps backward to his car and opening the trunk. "Show yourselves."

Three heads popped out of the trunk, those of a woman probably in her forties and two teenage girls.

Simon swallowed a sudden and intense hatred for the smuggler. He looked forward to taking him down so he could never take advantage of people like this ever again.

"Now the money." The guy sounded as if he was losing what little patience he had.

Carter tossed him the package. The smuggler flipped through the bills, and then he pulled out a pile of jewelry.

"What's this? I said cash."

"I didn't have time to sell it. But it's worth more than your price."

The guy shoved the jewelry back into the bag. "You know, now that I think about it, I want more."

"No, everything you asked for is there."

"But I can get more for your little lady's *familia* elsewhere."

When he moved to shut the trunk, Simon leveled his weapon at the guy and stepped out of the dark. "I wouldn't do that if I were you."

The guy pulled a gun as he spun toward Simon. "I said no cops."

"Simon, get out of here," Carter said.

"No chance."

Simon knew what Carter probably didn't, that the smuggler wasn't going to leave him alive to identify him. He was going to take the money and Josephina's family back to Mexico, and he'd sell them to the cartel. And Josephina's family would end up as dead as Carter. Simon couldn't allow either Josephina or Keri to have to mourn those losses. "Let them go."

"I have a gun, too," the guy said. "Maybe I shoot you first."

"You willing to bet your life on that?" The more this guy opened his mouth, the more Simon wanted to take him down.

The coyote motioned for his three captives to get out of the trunk. They scrambled out and started to stumble their way toward Carter. But then the guy made a quick move and pulled the youngest girl in front of him while taking aim at Simon's head. She cried out as Simon hit the ground and the guy fired. Everything happened so fast, and yet seemed to be in slow motion at the same time. Simon rolled into a crouch and fired at the smuggler as he pushed the girl away.

"No!" Simon yelled a moment after he pulled the trigger, when he saw the blur of Carter diving for the other guy. Another shot rang out and Carter's body jerked in midstride. Simon had no idea if it was his shot or the coyote's that hit Carter, or maybe both. All he knew is that Carter could not die.

Simon jumped to his feet and raced toward Carter. He got to him just as the other guy was trying to scramble to his feet. Simon punched the coyote so hard that he flew backward and was knocked out cold. He wasted no time flipping the guy onto his stomach and cuffing him. He resisted the nearly overpowering urge to slam his face against the ground. Instead, he turned to Carter, who was holding his side and trying to speak.

"Don't talk," Simon said as he ripped off his coat and pressed it against Carter's wound. He was vaguely aware of the cries of fear from Josephina's mother and sisters, but he couldn't pay any attention to them now.

Carter gripped Simon's arm. "Take care of Josephina, her family."

"Don't you worry about them. And stop talking."

Carter's eyes closed for a moment and his face contorted in pain. "Keri, help Keri."

"Damn it, man, you don't know when to listen, do you? Save your energy."

A cry and the sound of running feet drew Simon's attention. The sound of the shots must have drawn Josephina because she raced toward her family. She grabbed them in a group hug, then extricated herself as she spotted Carter on the ground.

"Carter." Her voice was so full of fear and pain that it twisted Simon's heart. She fell to her knees and framed Carter's face with her hands. "What have you done?"

"I'm sorry," Carter said.

The wail of sirens in the distance told Simon backup was on the way, but all he could focus on now was the hope that one of those sirens belonged to an ambulance.

Carter coughed and blood came out of his mouth. Simon cursed then leaned down close to Carter's face. "You listen to me, Carter Mehler. Fight, you hear me? Fight. Your sister has lost enough, and she's not going to lose you."

I don't want to lose you.

Carter looked up at him with a desperate need on his face. "You've got to help them. I'm begging you. Don't let them be deported."

Simon glanced at the approaching officers before meeting Carter's gaze again. "I'll do what I can."

The next several minutes were a blur as the medical personnel loaded Carter into the ambulance and immigration officials took Josephina's mother and sisters into custody. She looked so torn between her family and Carter, as though she might split in two.

Simon placed his hand on her shoulder. "Go with Carter. I'll take care of your family." He hoped he wasn't promising something he couldn't deliver.

Before he did anything, however, he had to make a phone call that he'd give everything not to make. A call that might prove to be the death knell to his relationship with Keri. Ironic that it would come on the heels of his realization that he loved her.

Chapter Fourteen

Keri still couldn't get her pounding heart under control even though she knew that Carter was out of surgery and the doctors were optimistic about his recovery. Still, he'd been shot. Shot!

And Simon had been the one to shoot him.

Her heart felt as if it was going to cleave in two.

If the evening had given her anything, however, it was the knowledge that Josephina did indeed love her brother. She'd refused to leave his side since he'd come out of surgery. She sat next to him, holding his hand and telling him how much she loved him, how brave she thought he was for going to save her family, how he had to get better because she needed him.

"I am sorry you are going through this," Josephina said to her. "After everything you have been through, you shouldn't have to see your brother like this."

"That's not your fault."

"It is, at least partly. He didn't have to help me."

Keri looked at the other woman and smiled. "I think he did. He told me that he loves you."

Josephina caressed Carter's hand. "I love him, too, with all my heart. I know he has had problems in the past, but he is a very good man."

Keri stared at a spot on the wall above Carter's head,

wondering how much more she could take before she simply fell apart and couldn't be put back together.

"Do you have someone special, someone you love?"

Keri knew what Josephina meant and closed her eyes. "Yes, but it doesn't matter anymore."

"How so?"

Keri glanced across at Josephina, who was watching her. "Because he's the one who shot Carter."

"Oh." Josephina started to say something else, but her eyes went to the door behind Keri.

When Keri looked over her shoulder, Simon stood in the doorway. Blood stained his uniform shirt. Carter's blood.

"Go away," she said, and turned back to face her brother's still form.

"How is he?"

Keri stood and stalked toward Simon, forcing him out into the corridor. "He'll live, no thanks to you."

"Keri—"

"No," she said as she poked her finger hard against his chest. "I asked you to bring him back safely, and you shot him. You could have killed him!"

"I know. Believe me, I know." He looked exhausted, drained, but she didn't have it in her to feel sorry for him. He wasn't the one who'd had to have a bullet dug out of his side, a bullet that had been fired by someone who was supposed to be a friend.

"Go home, Simon. I can't talk to you now."

He stared down at her for several seconds before nodding and turning slowly away. As he retreated down the corridor, tears streamed down her face. Despite everything, part of her wanted him to come back and pull her into his arms, to fight for her. Another part wanted to forget he even existed. She had no idea which part of her was going to win out in the end.

CHRISTMAS EVE ARRIVED, and Simon couldn't remember a holiday when he'd felt less merry. He missed Keri so much it felt as if his heart had taken a blast from a blowtorch. He knew his family was trying to keep things low-key out of respect for everything that had happened lately, but it was next to impossible to keep a lid on a good time when the entire Teague clan got together. And usually, he was right in the middle of it.

Today, he had to walk away. He headed outside and ended up down by the fence that looked out across the pasture. He'd kept his distance from Keri to give her as much time to think as she needed. But the more time passed, the more he worried that they'd come to the end of their relationship. And part of him understood that her focus was now on Hannah and Carter. She'd even given Josephina a job at the bakery and a place to stay in her home. He doubted he'd be welcome either place right now.

That didn't prevent him from keeping his promise to Carter, however. He'd done everything he could for Josephina's family, and now all he could do was cross his fingers.

"Tough day, huh?" his mom said as she walked up next to him.

"I've had better."

"I saw Keri yesterday. She seems to be doing well."

Part of him was happy with that news, but a very selfish part of him ached that she was evidently getting along fine without him.

"That's good."

"Well, but sad. Have you told that girl you love her?"

He sighed. "No. And I'm not sure I'll ever get the chance now."

"Then you make the chance."

Before he could respond that things weren't that simple, his phone rang. When he glanced at the number, his heart rate picked up. Please let this be good news. He took a few steps away from his mom before answering.

"Sheriff Teague."

As he listened to the words coming at him through the phone, he started to smile. By the time he ended the call, the day was suddenly looking a lot brighter.

"Good news, I take it," his mom said as he walked back toward her.

"Yes, very." At least it would be for Josephina and Carter. He didn't know if it would make any difference to Keri, but he planned to find out. He had to know if they had a future or not. He considered his next words before finally voicing them. "You remember how you once told me that someday when I needed it, I could have Great-grandma Opal's engagement ring?"

His mom smiled. "Yes."

"Well, I need it."

"I THINK SHE LIKES THE LIGHTS," Carter said as he lay on the couch next to where Hannah sat on the floor with her plastic blocks. He'd been building towers, and Hannah had been giggling as she knocked them over, for a good fifteen minutes as Keri and Josephina put the finishing touches on the Christmas tree.

Keri looked at the wide-eyed wonder on her niece's face and smiled. "Look how big her eyes are. I think she's mesmerized."

If not for Hannah, Keri doubted she would have decorated for Christmas this year. Carter was still recuperating and had an upcoming court date hanging over his head for the thefts, and the fate of Josephina's family was still up in the air.

And a hole had opened up in her heart where Simon used to be. Carter had noticed it and tried to talk her into calling Simon, even threatened to do it himself until she made him promise not to.

She'd been horrible to Simon at the hospital, before she'd known all the facts. She wouldn't be surprised if he never wanted to see her again. If nothing else, however, she had to get up the nerve to see him long enough to apologize.

Carter started building another tower of blocks, drawing Hannah's attention away from the Christmas tree. When she knocked over her uncle's creation before he was even halfway through, he feigned offense.

"Now, look what you've done. I think that calls for a tickle attack." Hannah laughed so loudly as Carter tickled her that Keri almost didn't hear the knock on the front door.

Who in the world would be coming to the door on Christmas Eve?

Her breath caught when she opened the door to see Simon standing there with his arms so full of presents she could only see the top half of his face.

"Ho ho ho," he said, sounding so much like his normal self that she couldn't help smiling.

Carter pushed himself off the couch and stepped up behind Keri. "Looks like Santa slimmed down some."

"Um, can Skinny Santa come in?"

Keri and Carter stepped to opposite sides of the path inside. Simon glanced at Keri, holding her eyes for a moment before heading for the tree.

Hannah smiled wide and clapped as she usually did when she saw him.

"Hey, how's my best girl?" he asked as he placed the presents under the tree. He bopped her nose playfully before standing to his full height.

The adults all stared at each other for several awkward moments. It was Josephina who spoke first.

"Would you like some hot chocolate?"

"Yes, thank you."

Unable to stand the tension any longer, Keri stepped forward. "Let me take your coat."

She'd swear she saw relief in his eyes as he shed both his coat and hat.

When Josephina returned from the kitchen with his hot chocolate and Keri turned around from placing his coat and hat in an empty chair, Simon was standing with his hand atop the pile of packages he'd brought.

"I know it's only Christmas Eve, but I'd like you all to open your presents now."

Keri and Carter exchanged surprised glances. She'd figured the entire stash was for Hannah. Simon did like to spoil her, after all.

He accepted his mug and took a quick sip before placing it on a side table. When he met Keri's gaze, she nodded.

After removing the smaller packages from the top, he scooted the biggest package toward Hannah.

"Wouldn't you know it?" Carter said. "Littlest person in the room gets the biggest present."

Simon laughed along with Carter. Keri knew the two of them had talked, that Simon had apologized for shooting Carter and Carter had done the same for putting himself and Simon in danger in the first place.

As she watched Simon, she held her breath at this tentative step toward…something better than what she'd been wading through the past several days.

When the big box was opened and the present was revealed to be a rocking horse, Keri had to laugh. "You really are going to try to turn her into a cowgirl."

"She'll be the best cowgirl in all of Texas," Simon said.

Keri's heart thumped a bit harder when she saw the obvious love on Simon's face for a little girl who wasn't even his, was no relation at all.

Next, Simon handed a box to Josephina.

"For me?" she asked in wide-eyed surprise.

He nodded, and she took the package. Other than Carter's recovery, she'd had so little to be happy about lately that it was good to see even the glimpse of holiday cheer on her face. But when she opened it, all that was inside was a piece of paper. As she read it, she gasped and placed her hand over her mouth.

"What is it?" Carter asked, but Josephina wasn't able to speak. Carter stepped close, wrapping his arm around her shoulders and reading the note for himself. When he looked up, astonishment was written across his face.

"What?" Keri asked.

Simon looked at her. "The feds have agreed to let Josephina's family stay in the country in exchange for all the information they have about the killing of that American boy in Mexico. His parents are both attorneys, and they have taken Josephina's mom and sisters under their wings. They're going to help them become citizens like Josephina."

"Oh, that's so wonderful."

Josephina stepped forward and wrapped her arms around Simon's waist. "Thank you."

Simon was caught off guard so it took him a moment to give her an awkward hug back.

When Simon handed Carter a box similar in size to Josephina's, Carter took it with a wary look.

"Please tell me there's not an arrest warrant in here because, I swear, Santa, I've been a good boy for several days now."

Simon gave Carter a crooked grin. "Only way to find out is to open it."

Carter made short work of the wrapping paper and opened the box. It also held a sheet of paper. Carter dropped the empty box on the couch and began to read. "This can't be right," he said after finishing.

"It is, every word."

"Why?"

"Isn't the end of one year and the beginning of the next the time for starting over?"

"Any other reason?" Carter asked.

Simon glanced at Keri. "Maybe."

"What the devil are you two being so cryptic about?" Keri asked.

Carter shifted his attention to his sister. "The charges against me have been dropped provided I pay back the value of everything I took. And…" Carter's voice broke before he managed to continue. "Simon's giving me a job at the ranch."

Keri pulled Carter into her arms and hugged him carefully with all the love a sister could have for a brother. When Carter backed out of the embrace, he looked at Simon. "I swear you won't be sorry. I'm done with the person I used to be." He shifted his gaze toward Josephina. "I'm a new man."

With gratitude overflowing for the happiness Simon had brought to her door, Keri crossed to him and hugged him close. "Thank you."

She felt the tension in him relax and wondered if he'd

worried he wouldn't be welcome in her home tonight. She'd given him no reason to think otherwise. What he didn't know was how very welcome he was, in her home, in her bed and in her heart. Somehow she had to find the perfect way to tell him.

"I'm sorry about before, at the hospital."

He rubbed his hand up and down her back. "No need to apologize."

When she tried to step back, he clasped her hand until she looked up at him.

"I still have your present."

She smiled. "I doubt seriously you can top what's already been given here tonight."

"I hope you're wrong." He reached into his pocket and started to descend to one knee.

Keri's heart jolted to attention as she realized what was happening. She bit her bottom lip as Simon held up a gold band topped by a small diamond.

"This was my great-grandmother's ring. My great-grandfather dug the diamond out of the earth himself up in Arkansas so he could give his future bride a ring he felt she deserved. And now I'm asking you, Keri Mehler, to accept it because I love you and I want you to be my wife. I want to help you raise Hannah. I'll even pitch in making a million pastries if that's what it takes to get you to say yes."

She stared at Simon and the ring, letting all the love she'd been holding back for fear she'd lose it flow out of the deepest part of her. She didn't realize how long she'd stood like that until Simon started to look worried.

"I have one condition," she said.

"Name it."

"You stick to horses and catching bad guys, and leave the pastries to me."

He smiled. "What? I thought I had a future as a pastry chef."

She screwed up her nose. "Not so much."

"Your wish is my command."

She smiled wide. "Then yes, Simon Teague, I will marry you because, as it happens, I love you, too."

Simon held her gaze as he slid the ring onto her finger then lifted to his feet and pulled her back into his arms. And then he sealed the deal with a kiss she'd swear shot sparks out of the ends of her toes. She was only vaguely aware of Carter's teasing whistle.

Pressure on her lower leg dragged her out of the kiss. When she looked down, Hannah was standing next to them with one hand on Keri's leg and one on Simon's.

"She walked." She hadn't since the couple of steps Keri had missed at Thanksgiving.

"Looks like it's a day for lots of new beginnings," Simon said as he scooped Hannah up in one of his arms.

As Keri held on to Simon and looked at the smiling faces of her brother and the woman who would no doubt someday be her sister-in-law, Keri's heart filled to bursting. She knew without a doubt that Sammi, Ben and her parents were there, too, smiling right along with everyone else.

She looked up at Simon. "I really do love you."

He smiled that flirty smile of his. "That's good news since you're stuck with me."

She couldn't imagine anyone better to be stuck with for the rest of her life.

* * * * *

HEART & HOME

Harlequin®

American ★ Romance®

COMING NEXT MONTH
AVAILABLE JUNE 12, 2012

#1405 BET ON A COWBOY
Julie Benson

#1406 RODEO DAUGHTER
Fatherhood
Leigh Duncan

#1407 THE RANCHER'S BRIDE
Pamela Britton

#1408 MONTANA DOCTOR
Saddlers Prairie
Ann Roth

You can find more information on upcoming Harlequin®
titles, free excerpts and more at www.Harlequin.com.

HARCNM0512

REQUEST YOUR FREE BOOKS!
2 FREE NOVELS PLUS 2 FREE GIFTS!

Harlequin®

American ★ Romance®

LOVE, HOME & HAPPINESS

YES Please send me 2 FREE Harlequin® American Romance® novels and my 2 FREE gifts (gifts are worth about $10). After receiving them, if I don't wish to receive any more books, I can return the shipping statement marked "cancel." If I don't cancel, I will receive 4 brand-new novels every month and be billed just $4.49 per book in the U.S. or $5.24 per book in Canada. That's a saving of at least 14% off the cover price! It's quite a bargain! Shipping and handling is just 50¢ per book in the U.S. and 75¢ per book in Canada.* I understand that accepting the 2 free books and gifts places me under no obligation to buy anything. I can always return a shipment and cancel at any time. Even if I never buy another book, the two free books and gifts are mine to keep forever.

154/354 HDN FEP2

Name _____ (PLEASE PRINT)

Address _____ Apt. #

City _____ State/Prov. _____ Zip/Postal Code

Signature (if under 18, a parent or guardian must sign)

Mail to the **Reader Service:**
IN U.S.A.: P.O. Box 1867, Buffalo, NY 14240-1867
IN CANADA: P.O. Box 609, Fort Erie, Ontario L2A 5X3

Not valid for current subscribers to Harlequin American Romance books.

**Want to try two free books from another line?
Call 1-800-873-8635 or visit www.ReaderService.com.**

* Terms and prices subject to change without notice. Prices do not include applicable taxes. Sales tax applicable in N.Y. Canadian residents will be charged applicable taxes. Offer not valid in Quebec. This offer is limited to one order per household. All orders subject to credit approval. Credit or debit balances in a customer's account(s) may be offset by any other outstanding balance owed by or to the customer. Please allow 4 to 6 weeks for delivery. Offer available while quantities last.

Your Privacy—The Reader Service is committed to protecting your privacy. Our Privacy Policy is available online at www.ReaderService.com or upon request from the Reader Service.

We make a portion of our mailing list available to reputable third parties that offer products we believe may interest you. If you prefer that we not exchange your name with third parties, or if you wish to clarify or modify your communication preferences, please visit us at www.ReaderService.com/consumerschoice or write to us at Reader Service Preference Service, P.O. Box 9062, Buffalo, NY 14269. Include your complete name and address.

HAR11B

SPECIAL EDITION

Life, Love and Family

USA TODAY bestselling author

Marie Ferrarella

enchants readers in

ONCE UPON A MATCHMAKER

Micah Muldare's aunt is worried that her nephew is going to wind up alone in his old age...but this matchmaking mama has just the thing! When Micah finds himself accused of theft, defense lawyer Tracy Ryan agrees to help him as a favor to his aunt, but soon finds herself drawn to more than just his case. Will Micah open up his heart and realize Tracy is his match?

Available June 2012

Saddle up with Harlequin® series books this summer and find a cowboy for every mood!

Available wherever books are sold.

www.Harlequin.com

HSE65674

*A grim discovery is about to change everything for
Detective Layne Sullivan—including how she
interacts with her boss!*

*Read on for an exciting excerpt of the upcoming book
UNRAVELING THE PAST by Beth Andrews....*

SOMETHING WAS UP—otherwise why would Chief Ross
Taylor summon her back out? As Detective Layne Sullivan
walked over, she grudgingly admitted he was doing well.
But that didn't change the fact that the Chief position
should have been hers.

Taylor turned as she approached. "Detective Sullivan,
we have a situation."

"What's the problem?"

He aimed his flashlight at the ground. The beam illuminated a dirt-encrusted skull.

"Definitely a problem." And not something she'd expected. Not here. "How'd you see it?"

"Jess stumbled upon it looking for her phone."

Layne looked to where his niece huddled on a log. "I'll
contact the forensics lab."

"Already have a team on the way. I've also called in units
to search for the rest of the remains."

So he'd started the ball rolling. Then, she'd assume command while he took Jess home. "I have this under control."

Though it was late, he was clean shaven and neat, his flat
stomach a testament to his refusal to indulge in doughnuts.
His dark blond hair was clipped at the sides, the top long
enough to curl.

The female part of Layne admitted he was attractive.

The cop in her resented the hell out of him for it.

"You get a lot of missing-persons cases here?" he asked.

"People don't go missing from Mystic Point." Although plenty of them left. "But we have our share of crime."

"I'll take the lead on this one."

Bad enough he'd come to *her* town and taken the position she was meant to have, now he wanted to mess with *how* she did her job? "Why? I'm the only detective on third shift and your second in command."

"Careful, Detective, or you might overstep."

But she'd never played it safe.

"I don't think it's overstepping to clear the air. You have something against me?"

"I assign cases based on experience and expertise. You don't have to like how I do that, but if you need to question every decision, perhaps you'd be happier somewhere else."

"Are you threatening my job?"

He moved so close she could feel the warmth from his body. "I'm not threatening anything." His breath caressed her cheek. "I'm giving you the choice of what happens next."

What will Layne choose? Find out in
UNRAVELING THE PAST by Beth Andrews,
available June 2012 from Harlequin® Superromance®.

And be sure to look for the other two books
in Beth's THE TRUTH ABOUT THE SULLIVANS series
available in August and October 2012.

Harlequin® Romance

A touching new duet from fan-favorite author

SUSAN MEIER

First Time **DADS!**

When millionaire CEO Max Montgomery spots
Kate Hunter-Montgomery—the wife he's never forgotten—
back in town with a daughter who looks just like him, he's
determined to win her back. But can this savvy business tycoon
convince Kate to trust him a second time with her heart?

Find out this June in
THE TYCOON'S SECRET DAUGHTER

And look for book 2 coming this August!
NANNY FOR THE MILLIONAIRE'S TWINS

Saddle up with Harlequin® series books this summer
and find a cowboy for every mood!